Shadow Jumper

J M Forster

Cover design by Mark Fox

www.jm-forster.co.uk

www.jm-forster.com

To Ben, Louis and Giles.

With love.

Chapter One

Jack was trying hard not to die. One wrong move and he'd lie splattered on the pavement or fried to a crisp by the sun. He knew the risks, but the roof was the one place he could taste real freedom.

Pressing his back into the shadows of the tall chimney stacks, he ran his fingers through his oil-coated hair and shook the mass of worm-like tendrils. Then he flipped up his hood. Even though the sun had almost set, the searing heat pierced the thick fabric, stabbing the crown of his head. A bead of sweat tickled its way towards his chin. The slimy oil he'd slapped on earlier stuck his shirt to his chest. He flapped it back and forth, trying to generate a current of air to cool his itchy body.

A sharp pain radiated along the back of his hand. He inspected the bleeding crack, smearing a droplet of blood with his thumb. His skin was getting worse. Dad would know what to do, but by the time he decided to come home . . . well, anything could have happened.

Jack normally stopped thinking about Dad for a short time when on the roofs. But not today. He sighed heavily. Since when had life got so complicated? Scrap that; *his* life had always been complicated – Dad's absence added one more problem to the long list.

He shielded his eyes with his hand and squinted at the view – he never got tired of it. He could see over the tops of the Victorian grey slated roofs to the cathedral in the west of the city. The tower glinted where the sunlight hit the golden brickwork. Not far in the opposite direction, he made out the square apartment block where he lived, its greyness merging with the other dirty anonymous buildings. The sounds from the streets below – the roar of traffic and beeps from car horns – were muffled. The only real noise came from the birds calling to each other as they circled lazily overhead.

And then his phone buzzed. He rooted in his pocket and brought it out. One new message popped up on the screen. From Mum.

How r u? Beans in fridge 4 t

That meant she'd be late back from work again that night. He tapped in his reply.

OK

He pressed **Send** and slid the phone back in his trouser pocket. She always complained his replies were too short. But what else could he say?

Hi Mum. On roof. About to jump. Beans 4 t fine

He didn't think that would go down too well.

The shadows were lengthening. Jack checked the laces on his trainers and got to his feet, taking care not to slip on the smooth tiles. He cast a look around him at the familiar spot; he'd chosen the perfect playground to practise his urban acrobatics. The shapes and angles created by the old city roofs — the steep pitches with terracotta clay ridges along the peaks, and the gentler, easy slopes — were brilliant for what he had in mind. He studied the distances between the shadows made by the chimneys, searching for where he'd place his feet. He was ready.

He took a couple of deep breaths and shook his arms to relax the taut muscles. Then he stepped forwards and jumped, one leg stretched in front of the other, like an athlete soaring over hurdles, his eyes fixed on their target. For a fleeting moment his body filled to bursting with a tingling thrill before he landed with a grunt in a narrow band of shade.

He steadied himself, one hand on the wall of a

chimney, and looked for his next secure place. Then he set off again, somersaulting over low ledges and scrambling up a steep pitch. At the top, he bounced off a chimney wall, twisting in the air to change direction.

As he touched down on the slates, his foot slipped. His arms windmilled as he tried to stop himself tumbling. The next instant he was on his back, slithering at high speed towards the guttering. He scrabbled about, trying to gain a foothold. His body was out of control, hurtling relentlessly downwards.

He slid faster and faster. The sheer drop loomed below him. A wave of panic swept over him as he careered towards it, fingers sliding uselessly off the slates. A sob rose in his throat. He didn't want to die, but it really did feel like the end. Any second now he'd plunge off the edge.

"Aaaaah!" he yelled as he came to a sudden stop. His top must have snagged on a nail or something because he was now suspended with his shirt rucked up around his chest, the gathered fabric slicing into his armpits. His legs dangled over the edge of the roof.

"Calm down," he said to himself, taking a few deep breaths. "You're okay."

His body ached all over but he needed to pull himself together. His next move would either save him or create a crumpled, messy heap in the street below. If he could just see what his shirt was caught on.

Shakily, he twisted his head around.

And then he started to scream.

Chapter Two

Glaring down at Jack was a ghostly white face, surrounded by a mass of jet-black, spiky hair. The face had a wide, black mouth and enormous dark eyes.

Spots swam in front of Jack's eyes. He squeezed them shut, willing himself not to faint. The blood pulsed and hammered inside his head.

"Stop screeching and give me your hand!"

His eyes snapped open again. The figure gritted its teeth, its black lips parting and stretching into two thick parallel lines. It crouched on the roof, feet planted above him, leaning backwards, as it held onto his shirt with both hands. As the figure tugged harder, the stretched material bunched up around Jack's armpits and neck. His chafed flesh stung and he heard an ominous ripping as his shirt

6

started to tear.

"Quick. I can't hold on . . ."

With immense effort, Jack stretched upwards. A cool hand gripped his oiled, slippery fingers and pulled. For one hopeless moment, he thought there was *no way* it would be able to save him. But then it reached down with its other hand, letting go of his top and clutching his sleeved arm. With one hand followed by the other, as if pulling on a rope, it heaved him upwards. Tug by agonising tug, it hauled him away from the edge, his back scraping across the tiles and bumping over the ridges.

His whole body safely back on the roof, Jack flopped onto the tiles, trembling from shock. He closed his eyes, trying to ease the panicky sensation fizzing in the depths of his stomach.

"Lucky I was here."

Opening his eyes once more he turned towards the voice. Relief flooded his tense body. It was a girl; he could see that now. Her face was plastered with black and white make-up. She lay on her back gazing up at the sky, rubbing her right arm.

His throat contracted as if a massive ball of dust clogged his airway. He gave a tiny swallow. He'd never been so close to death before. "Th . . . thanks."

"You shouldn't be up here," the girl continued. "You're

far too young to be running around on roofs."

He was trying hard to calm down after his near-death experience, but a tiny spark of annoyance flared up inside him. *He* was too young? If she thought wearing black make-up and clothes made her look older than him, then she was so wrong. Perhaps best, though, if he didn't tell her she looked like she'd stepped out of a horror film. She had saved his life after all.

"I was shadow jumping," he mumbled.

"What's that?"

"A game. Jumping between the shadows." There was nothing like having to explain why he liked being on a roof to make him feel a prize idiot. "It stops me getting bored."

"Yeah, that would banish the boredom," she said. "Being dead."

"I'm normally more careful." Jack couldn't help shuddering at the memory of helplessly slipping down the roof. "But, I've got some things on my mind."

"I know the feeling. I actually thought you were brilliant. A bit mad, though. I wish I could do it," she said. "I'm Beth, by the way."

"Jack. So, what are you doing up here?" he asked, attempting to sound offhand.

Her white cheeks went as red as his top. "I saw you in

the street. And you were kind of acting strangely. Then you disappeared up the alley, so I followed you."

He propped himself up on his elbows so he could look at her properly. She lay next to him: thin, pale arms and legs peeked out from her black T-shirt and leggings. A silver-buckled belt looped around her narrow waist. He wondered how those skinny limbs had the strength to drag him up the roof. A bulky, black rucksack sat on the tiles next to her.

"I wanted to find out what you were up to," she continued.

Jack couldn't believe it. He'd been tailed by a girl who looked like a cross between a vampire and a zombie because she thought *he* looked strange.

"Now you know." Jack was feeling more uncomfortable by the minute. How come he hadn't noticed her?

"Then I saw you slip, so I reached out and grabbed . . ."

"I was fine – still in control."

The girl's black eyebrows shot up her forehead in a "stop messing – we both know I saved you from certain death" way. Or that's what it seemed like to Jack. He stared back, hoping his face said, "If you tell anyone about this, I will hunt you down and rip those eyebrows off your face." But he probably looked like a grimacing baboon.

Before he'd managed to rearrange his features, Beth had scrabbled to her feet and hitched the rucksack onto her shoulder.

"I gotta go," she said. "See you around." She started picking her way back over the shiny tiles and clambering up the sloping roof, glancing back once to say, "No more mad tricks."

Jack gazed after her, mouth hanging open. The last thing he needed was some weird girl telling him what to do. But before he had time to let rip, she'd disappeared over the ridge.

He sighed and shook his shoulders. The muscles had bunched painfully from tension. His mind was filled with a never-ending spiral of twitchy thoughts. Slipping down the roof like that hadn't helped. Time out. That's what he needed. A rest from a skin allergy that meant every time he stepped into the sun, he risked being scorched like an overcooked sausage on a barbeque. And he wanted a dad who stayed at home when he needed him most.

He scrambled to his feet, aware the sun had dipped behind the neighbouring roofs. It would soon be getting dark. As he was about to jump down onto a red brick wall, something white caught his eye. It was wedged in the gutter amongst the dead leaves and moss, but it hadn't been there on his way up, he was sure of that.

Curious, he hunkered down to take a closer look. It was a piece of thick, white paper, crumpled and worn at the edges. He picked it up and went to turn it over. A clattering made him glance up and a piece of slate skittered past his head, too close for comfort. Without thinking, Jack shoved the paper in his pocket and stood up quickly.

"Hello?" he called out. Every nerve in his body was jangling, and his scalp tingled as if someone was watching him. But when he scanned the rooftops there was no one there.

Chapter Three

As usual, nosy Mrs Roberts popped her head around her door as he put his key in the lock. She had an uncanny knack of hearing him coming – how did she do that when she was supposed to be as deaf as a lump of wood?

"Everything all right?" she cackled, displaying a set of stumpy, greying teeth.

"Fine, thank you, Mrs Roberts," he shouted, making sure he kept his distance from her smelly mouth. "I'm going to get something to eat!"

"Sore feet?" She glanced down at her pink fluffy slippers. "Yes, they are a little painful."

"No, not sore feet," shouted Jack. "Something to eat!"

"Oh, right." She looked confused for a second. "But I've had my supper already. Well, perhaps I could do with some crackers and cheese. Night, night."

She shuffled backwards and disappeared inside her flat. Jack sighed and opened his door.

"Mum?" Silence. He'd forgotten she'd still be at work. He heated up a huge panful of baked beans, toasted two slices of bread and wolfed them down standing by the sink. Sauce dribbled down his chin and plopped into the washing-up bowl. Jack could almost hear Mum tutting with annoyance as he stood there, but at least it saved on the washing-up.

He glanced at the clock: past ten already. There was no point waiting up for Mum, she could be ages. He showered to wash the grease off his skin and hair and collapsed on the bed. His body was weary but his mind restless. His stuffy bedroom didn't help. He tossed back his duvet, knelt on the bed and yanked up the blind. Then he opened the window as far as it would go. He flopped onto his back, and watched the strange, elongated shadows created by light from the street dancing on his ceiling.

He must have dozed off because he came to a while later with the sound of Mum clattering about in the kitchen which was next to his room. He slipped out of bed.

She was sitting at the table, with a cup of tea.

"Fancy one?" She gestured at the kettle. A wispy plume of steam still hovered in the air above it.

He shook his head and sank into the chair opposite.

"What's the matter with your hand?"

He gulped and whipped it under the kitchen table. If she realised his skin was getting worse she'd ban him from going outside altogether. "I scratched myself. It's nothing."

He glanced at her face, wondering if she'd quiz him about it. Dark circles surrounded each eye; they'd been there since she and Dad split up four months ago.

"There's antiseptic in the bathroom cabinet." She heaved herself up, rinsed her mug under the tap and placed it on the draining board, pushing a floppy strand of brown hair from her brow as she did so.

"Dad hasn't called then?" he said, crushing his sore hand between his knees to stop the unbearable itch.

"Sorry, love, no."

"Typical," he grunted.

Mum shot him a disapproving look but she didn't disagree. Instead she mumbled something that sounded like "Too busy thinking about himself." Then in a louder voice she said, "Your dad finds it easy to forget what really matters. But it's not been that long since we heard from him."

14

Jack thought three weeks was plenty long enough. His birthday – that's when Dad sent the email. And no present, no card, no phone call. Nothing. Mum said he didn't like mobile phones and that's why he hadn't rung. That seemed like such a feeble excuse. Hadn't he heard of a phone box? And where was he? He hadn't visited for months.

Mum smoothed down the stray strand of hair that threatened to fall in front of her eyes again. "Things are tricky at the moment for him, but I'm sure once he's found a permanent job and is settled in one place, he'll get in touch."

"Why did you chuck him out then, if it's so tough for him?" Jack ground the heel of each hand into his tired eyes.

"We've been through this before, Jack. It was a joint decision for him to leave. I couldn't take . . ."

Jack jerked his head up as Mum's words tailed off. "What?"

She rubbed her brow. "It's too late for this conversation now. If it'll make you feel better, I'll make a few phone calls and see if I can find anything else out. Okay? But right now you need to go to bed."

She ushered him from the room. But he knew he wouldn't be able to sleep, so he sneaked back into the hall and, crouching down, pressed his ear to the sitting room door, listening as she made call after call. At last, with the muscles in his legs screaming to be released, Jack could take it no longer. He tiptoed back to bed, a blanket of misery surrounding him. What a waste of time. Nobody had a clue where Dad was. And if Mum couldn't find him, what would happen to his skin? He flopped back onto the pillow and shut his eyes, trying to block the surge of hopelessness that washed over him.

Chapter Four

The next evening, Jack was back on the roofs. The sun, already low, peeped between the chimney stacks. The violent orange sky bled into the darkening clouds, creating a cluster of purple bruises. Long shadows surrounded Jack, as he hopped onto a ledge and surveyed the collection of rooftops. He'd been waiting all day for this moment and he planned to savour every precious minute of it.

Exactly ten seconds later he spotted something out the corner of his eye. Or rather someone. A huddled figure wearing black. Beth was sitting with her back to one of the tallest chimneys, her rucksack by her side. Seeing her made his nerves jangle. Was she stalking him? Then he noticed her head was buried in her arms and her shoulders were juddering up and down.

Jack hesitated. He needed someone else's problems like a hole in the head. But he couldn't very well leave her there looking so upset. He slowly made his way towards the hunched shape. He put out a hand and touched her lightly on the shoulder. She practically jumped out of her skin.

"Why did you sneak up on me?" she squawked, rubbing her eyes frantically. The smudged black and white make-up tinged her face a ghoulish grey.

"Sorry," he said. "Are you okay?"

"Do I look okay?"

He shrugged and started to turn away. If she was going to be like that, he really couldn't be bothered with her. He had better things to do with his time, like shadow jumping.

"If you must know, I've lost something," she said. "Satisfied?"

His heart thumped uncomfortably against his chest wall. Dealing with a bawling goth girl wasn't what he had in mind when he left the flat earlier.

"Sorry," he said again. He shifted uncomfortably from one foot to the other and waited for her to say more. But all she did was take another swipe at her tears and then stare at him.

"You've cut yourself."

He glanced down at the angry-looking sore on back of his hand. It extended from the bony base of his forefinger to his wrist. A brown, crusty scab had formed over the top, but he must have knocked it on his way up. Now blood seeped onto the pink, raw-looking skin skirting around the edges of the wound. It looked revolting.

"Here. You've got to keep it clean." Beth produced a bottle out of her rucksack. He winced as she poured water over the gash. Then she rummaged in her bag again, bringing out what looked like a mini first-aid kit, tore open a small carton and carefully covered the wound with a plaster. "I told you it's dangerous running around on roofs."

"I didn't do it on the roof."

Beth handed him her water bottle and he took a swig.

"You're not going to leave me hanging are you?" She leant forwards and peered at his face underneath his hood. "Is it something to do with this gunk you're covered with?"

Jack nodded. Before he knew it, everything tumbled out in a rush. It was as if someone had shaken him up like a bottle of fizzy drink and then unscrewed the cap. Words exploded out of his mouth at a force he couldn't stop – weeks, months of silent worry released in a torrent – all about being allergic to sunlight and wearing the horrible gooey gloop to stop his skin burning.

"Oh, I've read about that," said Beth. "In a magazine. What's it called? Photo . . . something."

"Photosensitivity." Jack normally didn't like talking about his condition. Whenever he did, people would listen for a few seconds and then slink away, as if afraid what he had was catching. To his relief, Beth wasn't like that. There were no sudden excuses to leave. No furtive wiping of her hands as if she'd touched something repulsive. She listened, asked questions and that was all.

"I've had it since I was a baby," he said, examining the plaster. "The doctors have tried everything – but I'm allergic to all their treatments. My dad's a research scientist and made up a special sun lotion for me to use – super-strong stuff but good for my skin. It buys me time – extra minutes I can be in the sun without burning." As he spoke, an intense prickliness spread along his wounded hand and misery washed over him. "Now it's stopped working, my skin condition's gone crazy and Dad's left home. I've no idea where he is."

"Why don't you go and find him?" said Beth, getting to her feet and heaving her rucksack onto her back. "Before it's too late. I'll help you, if you like," she called, glancing at him over her shoulder. "I haven't got anything

20

else to do over the summer."

Jack trailed behind her. "N . . . no, it's okay." Unease pulsed through him. He wasn't used to people being friendly towards him, especially when he'd just met them. And he wasn't sure Dad wanted to be found.

"What's the problem?" Beth stopped and twisted round to stare at him.

"Nothing," he said, wishing now he hadn't opened his big mouth and told her his problems.

"Look, you're not the only one who's bored. I moved here a couple of weeks ago; you're the first person I've met. You need help to find your dad and I'm offering it. But if you don't want it . . ." Beth looked at him, hands placed on her hips, like Mum stood when she was cross about something.

What could he say? He didn't know her well enough to spend any time with her? That sounded really weak. How else could he get to know people unless he spent time with them? She scared him? That was plain pathetic. He moaned about not having any friends and here was someone offering friendship. Why wasn't he jumping at the chance? Because he was an idiot. He opened his mouth to speak but Beth got there before him.

"The least you can do is teach me how to shadow jump," she said. "You owe me."

Jack inhaled sharply. "No way."

She'd saved his life and listened to his problems, sure, but the roofs were *his* safe place. Shadow jumping was *his* thing. He didn't feel ready to share it with anyone. He scoured his mind for an excuse, a reason he could give that would get her to drop the subject. "It takes tons of practice. And strength."

"You think I'm not strong enough?"

He remembered her clutching his arm and hauling him away from the edge of the roof. A ripple of heat rose up his cheeks.

"If you can do it, so can I," she said.

"That's different."

"How?" asked Beth, her voice cool.

He didn't reply.

Five minutes later he was crouching with Beth at the bottom of one of the steep pitches. The ornate chimneys that dominated the Victorian skyline towered above them.

"You won't be able to jump with that on your back," he said, jerking a thumb at her rucksack. "It'll weigh you down."

"I'm used to it. It's coming with me." Beth's black eyes flashed.

He shrugged. She'd have to find out for herself. He set off to perform a series of moves she could copy.

He darted up a steep pitch, stopping in the shadow of a chimney stack. Then he slid downwards, using the parapet to brake against at the bottom. Twisting round, he watched Beth slithering towards him, her mouth open in a wide "O" of surprise. He sprinted towards the next patch of shade. In front of him the roof flattened out and a red brick wall reared up, casting a giant shadow. He dashed forwards, jumping and rotating at the same time. His right foot kicked off the wall and propelled him over the low barrier to his left. Then with both arms extended he vaulted over a concrete block, his hands driving him forwards. He stopped the other side, waiting for Beth to catch him up.

"That's such a rush," she panted, as she leapt over to join him in the shadows. Her hair drooped in front of her eyes and she impatiently pushed it aside. "And you're brilliant at it."

He looked away. He'd secretly hoped that she'd hate shadow jumping. Typical of his luck she loved it.

They clambered up the wall separating the roof from its neighbour and dropped down the other side. A couple of striped deckchairs and an upside-down crate were set out on the flat roof to make a crude terrace. The sun had almost set now. Long shadows stretched from the building across the makeshift patio. Behind was a large sash window, the bottom pane thrown up. Several lager cans littered the area surrounding the seats and faint laughter mixed with music drifted out from the building.

"Come on." To Jack's dismay she made for the nearest chair and plonked herself down, bringing out her water bottle from her rucksack. She shook it at him. "What you waiting for?"

He edged over and pulled the deckchair further into the shade, flicking a look at the window.

"Relax, we'll move if they come out here," she said. She took a sip of water. "Why don't you tell your mum about your skin? She could help you find your dad. Or get another doctor to take a look at it."

Jack snorted. "I'm fed up with doctors poking and prodding me and being a guinea pig for their new medicines. Besides, she'll know soon enough. If it gets too bad, I won't be able to hide it—"

"Who're you?"

Jack flinched at the harsh voice. A head appeared at the window and a boy with cropped brown hair glared down at him, his mouth twisted into a sneer. His forehead bulged; thick brows hung over his eyes, which were dark sunken dots in his face. Broad shoulders jutted out at right angles from his jaw, his neck made invisible by his muscular frame. He looked older than them, maybe sixteen or seventeen. Whatever his age, he was huge.

Jack scrambled to his feet, pulling Beth up beside him. He licked his lips which had become sandpaper dry. A sick sensation bubbled up from the pit of his stomach. "We're just leaving."

The boy ducked through the window. He strutted towards them and then stopped as he stared first at Jack and then at Beth, his lip curling in disgust.

"What's with the face?" he asked Beth, rudely.

"What's with yours?" she retorted.

"How did you get up here?" The boy glanced up as if they'd fallen from the sky.

"What's it to you?" said Beth. Jack put a warning hand on her arm. Her body quivered under his touch.

"This ain't your roof, so clear off." The boy took a step towards her. Instinctively Jack took a pace back, dragging Beth by the arm. He cast a sidelong look at her face. It was blank, but a tiny pulse pounded in her jaw. And her hands were clenched into tight balls.

The music from inside stopped and a female voice pierced the silence. "Kai! Where are you? I've found more beer."

Jack jerked Beth's arm. "Let's go."

"Nobody pushes me around," she said.

"He's got a point, though. This is his roof."

Beth snorted, but allowed him to lead her back the way they'd come. As they scrambled onto the top of the wall Jack looked back. The boy called Kai was still standing on the terrace glaring up at them.

"Er, Beth, time to run," he said, as Kai suddenly shifted in their direction.

Jack didn't wait to see whether Kai would be able to scale the wall. He leapt off it. Landing with bended knees, he rolled using his right shoulder to propel him to his feet. Beth landed awkwardly beside him.

"Go back to the warehouse roof," he panted. "I'll head him off."

He watched Beth disappear up the next ridge and waited. Seconds later a face appeared at the top of the wall. Jack turned away and hurtled in the opposite direction to Beth. He swung under a metal bar, hurdled a low wall and scampered up an incline. Sharp yells from the boy pursued him. He ducked behind a chimney stack. The blood in his veins buzzed from the thrill of the chase. Beads of sweat covered his face; he wiped them away with his sleeve.

Popping his face around the stack he saw Kai. He was standing below looking around, his heavy brow creased in a frown. Jack smiled. No doubt he thought he'd disappeared into thin air. He waited. Then, hearing no more, he got to his feet and made his way back to the warehouse roof.

"I lost him," he said, sinking onto the tiles. His stretched muscles throbbed.

"Sorry 'bout overreacting. I hate bullies," said Beth. "But the jumping was so much fun. Can we do it again?"

"It's too late. And I've had enough," said Jack, weariness suddenly swathing him like a thick cloak. He'd got a kick out dealing with Kai, but he could still be lying in wait for them somewhere. And Beth's fieriness had sapped his energy. She seemed to go out of her way to pick a fight while he avoided it.

As they made their way back across the roofs, uneasy thoughts twisted and collided inside his head. The roofs had been his bolthole. A place to retreat when life got tough. When his skin was driving him crazy and he needed to escape the flat. But a line had been crossed when he and Beth had jumped that first shadow together. It meant sharing his refuge with her. And now she'd attracted the attention of Kai, who knew how safe it was to be up there any more?

But Jack was fed up with being lonely. For years he'd wanted friendship, and Beth offered it – along with her fierce temper and impulsive nature.

"Look, do you want to come by my place tomorrow, to hang out?" he blurted, before he had a chance to change his mind.

Beth shrugged. "Thought you didn't want anything to do with me."

"Sorry about that. I'm not used to people being so friendly."

Beth shrugged again as if she couldn't care less and then sighed. "Life's too short."

Jack was about to ask her what she meant when a small smile appeared on her face, her black lips curling up at the edges.

"Cathy said something about shopping for school uniform, but I'll sneak out before she catches me."

"Who's Cathy?" asked Jack. "Your mum?"

There was a pause. Beth started to look uncomfortable.

"Er, not quite. There's something you should know about me."

Chapter Five

When Beth said both her parents were dead, Jack felt strangely relieved. Given the way she looked, he'd been half-expecting her to say they were werewolves or vampires or members of some weird cult.

"Er . . . sorry." It was a pretty dumb thing to say, he knew, but he couldn't think of anything better.

"It's okay. It was two years ago. I'm over it."

Jack glanced at her in surprise. He couldn't imagine ever getting over it if his parents died. And if she was all right about it, he wondered why she looked so edgy.

"They died in a car crash. It was a head-on collision with a lorry. They were killed instantly." Beth's tone was flat and expressionless, but she kept twisting the straps of her rucksack around her fingers. "I live with my parents' friends now. They're my legal guardians."

"That must be tough," said Jack.

"It's okay. Lonely, though."

"So that's why you follow strangers down the street to see what they're up to," said Jack, trying to lighten the mood a little.

"Good job I did," she was quick to reply.

Jack grinned, relieved the awkward moment had passed. He still didn't understand, though, why she looked so uneasy when talking about her parents. It couldn't have been the first time she'd had to tell a stranger about their deaths.

"Cathy and Pete are lovely to look after me, so I don't have to go into care. But it's not like having real parents."

"Don't you have any other family?"

"Nope. Only a distant cousin of my dad and she didn't want anything to do with me."

Jack jumped nimbly onto a red brick wall and then to the ground. He stood by a large green rubbish bin, near the entrance of the gloomy alley. Something crunched underneath his shoe. He bent down to have a look. The remains of a mobile phone lay at his feet. He picked up a couple of the pieces and groaned, feeling in his pocket. Empty. It must have dropped out when he was running from Kai. Mum would kill him. He stuffed the pieces into his pocket, not sure how he would explain its condition to Mum when he got home. It would take ages to save up for a new one. Not that he cared; he didn't use it much.

They had reached the noisy main street. The narrow pavement was jam-packed with jostling workers and tourists spilling out of bars and restaurants. The sticky heat from the masses of people and buildings seared through Jack's thick clothes. His skin prickled as if an army of ants was crawling in his flesh.

He and Beth fought their way through the throng to find a quieter spot to talk. In the end they dipped into the doorway of a closed sandwich shop and watched the crowd stream past. Jack started digging in his pocket for something to write with. Keys, a used tissue and the bits of his phone tumbled onto his hand. Impatiently, he pushed them back in.

"Here." Beth opened a zipped compartment of her rucksack. She handed him a pen, held out her hand and he wrote his address on it.

Beth opened her mouth as if to say something, but then took back her pen and made to leave.

"Don't forget this." Jack went to pick up the rucksack but found his fingers closing around thin air. He looked up in surprise.

"I don't like people touching my bag," snapped Beth,

as she clutched the straps and stuffed the pen back in its compartment.

With a curt wave, Beth set off jogging down the street. He watched until she became swallowed up by the swarming people. "What was that about?" he wondered to himself, as made his way back to the flat in the opposite direction.

*

The next morning started with good news. Auntie Lil had phoned to say Dad had got a new job on a science project. But Jack groaned with frustration when he found out Mum still didn't know where he was.

"Where's your phone?" said Mum, as she dashed around, getting her things ready for work. "Your dad tried to call but he couldn't get through. And what with me on the phone, he couldn't get through here either. He's promised to ring again in a couple of weeks when things have settled down."

With a flash of guilt, Jack remembered the broken phone pieces lying in his bedroom. Luckily Mum was too busy droning on about "patching things up", it being "for the best" and "four months being a long time" to ask any more. His attention drifted.

Would Dad really ring in a fortnight? He didn't have a good track record of keeping promises. And Jack couldn't afford to wait days let alone weeks. The sores were popping up at a faster rate than ever. A new patch of inflamed skin had appeared overnight behind his right ear. He'd had to brush his hair forwards to hide it from Mum. The latest bumpy blotch was only five or six millimetres across, but at the rate things happened to his body, it could be colossal by the end of the day. It was as if the allergy had gone berserk. He couldn't bear to think what might happen if he didn't get help. Would his skin drip off his body, like melting candle wax?

"Are you listening to me, Jack?"

Jack looked at her blankly.

"I wanted you to know how things stand between us, and then everyone's clear. No secrets, right?"

He nodded vaguely.

"So what's this important thing you need to tell him?"

He hesitated. If he told her about his skin, she'd make him stay inside with Mrs Roberts watching him like a hawk. There'd be no more shadow jumping. And she'd probably make him go back to the doctor for more useless tests and medication.

"Nothing. I'd just like to see him."

Mum ruffled his hair. "I know, love. You have to be patient. I'm off to work. Mrs Roberts will pop in at lunchtime."

He groaned. He didn't need a childminder – he was fourteen after all. And he was convinced that Mrs Roberts spied on him, with her little beady eyes.

Mum turned away and picked up her bag. "Remember—"

"My lotion, I know." He rolled his eyes. She said the same thing every day.

"I wish I could take you on holiday somewhere. But with money so tight at the moment, and me doing double shifts at the supermarket—"

"Mum, stop fussing," he snapped. But his irritation instantly faded when he glanced at her face. Hurt was etched in the lines creasing her brow. "There's no point me going on holiday," he continued more gently. "Not the way I am."

Mum reached out a hand and placed it on his forehead. Her touch, usually cool and soothing on his skin, annoyed him today. "It's not much fun for you, is it, being stuck inside in this heat?" she said. "And in the school holidays, too."

Jack's face grew hot. A good job Mum had no idea how he spent his time, or she'd never let him out of her sight. "Um. Don't worry, I've got something to do. A mate's coming over."

"Great! Who is he?"

"She," said Jack awkwardly, hoping Mum wouldn't make a big deal out of it. "Beth's going to be at my school next term."

"I'm glad you've made a friend," said Mum smoothly. "I know things have been difficult for you."

"Mum! Don't make me sound so sad."

She was right though; school was a nightmare. He couldn't play sports outside like everyone else or go out at lunchtime because of his condition. Instead he spent his time cooped up in the computer room or library, staying well away from the large windows. And because he didn't do the same things the others did, finding mates sometimes seemed like an impossible challenge. His stomach tightened as he remembered those times he'd started new schools and tried to make friends. At one place kids shunned him because they were scared of catching "Slime Disease". At another he'd earned the nickname "Oil Slick". Used to being ignored, he'd learnt to keep himself to himself. That meant with girls too. No one in their right mind would hold hands with him, let alone do anything else.

He'd lost count of the number of times he'd wished Dad would get a job and stick with it. Was it really so hard to stay working at the same place for more than nine months? Then he wouldn't have to keep going through the torture of starting somewhere new. The one good thing about Dad leaving was, for the first time in ages, Jack would start the new academic year at the same school as last term.

"Mum?"

"What, love?"

He hesitated. "Have a good day!"

She looked at him quizzically. "You too."

Desperation swept over him as the door slammed and he was left to his own thoughts. He was right not to mention his problems – Mum's overprotective streak was bad enough as it was. He had no choice – he'd have to sort this out himself. But loneliness smothered him like the lotion he rubbed into his skin.

Chapter Six

As Jack waited for Beth in the corridor outside the flat, he noticed Mrs Robert's door was open a crack. A pink slippered foot jutted out through the gap and he glimpsed a wisp of grey hair and an eye peering at him.

"Afternoon!" he called. Couldn't he do anything without her interfering?

Mrs Roberts muttered something and slammed the door. Oops, she couldn't read his mind as well, could she? He didn't have time to dwell on that further, though, because Beth came bounding up the stairs.

"Wow!" she said as she nudged past him and entered the flat. "How many of you live in here?"

"Me and my mum. Why?"

"It's so . . . compact."

Jack glanced around as if seeing the flat for the first time. The front door opened straight into the living room that had enough space for a sofa, armchair and small TV stand. Scuff marks covered the dirty yellow paintwork. A gas fire clung to one wall, looking as if one tug would pull it off. Even when it was cold, Mum refused to switch it on, worried they'd die from lethal fumes. A wilting plant sat on a table under the burgundy curtains – not enough light penetrated through the narrow window to keep it happy. A hallway off the living room led to the two pokey bedrooms, a narrow kitchen–diner and a minute bathroom. Actually "bathroom" was too grand a word to use for the cupboard crammed in between the bedrooms, housing a shower, toilet and basin.

"Mum likes being in the city centre. Lots of people around."

He grimaced as he took in the saggy old furniture; even though Mum had hung a few pictures to cheer the place up, it was still grotty. But it was all they could afford. He'd never been able to call it home – it didn't feel like one.

"We're renting it until Mum and Dad get back together," he continued. Why did he have the urge to apologise? "Then we'll buy somewhere."

"You think they'll get back together?" Beth raised an

eyebrow.

"Yeah." He sounded defensive. The truth was he didn't want to contemplate any other outcome. His mind flitted back to before Mum and Dad split up, to the overheard arguments, Mum calling Dad "selfish" and "unreliable", Dad stomping around, slamming doors. All parents fought, didn't they? What bothered him more was Dad's disappearing act.

Beth sauntered around looking at photos placed on top of the TV and picking up Mum's ornaments. Jack hovered next to her, not sure what to say or do.

"What's the place like where you live?" he asked eventually, fed up with watching Beth inspect his belongings.

"Oh, you know – big house, huge garden. Eight kids. None my age though."

"Eight!" He couldn't begin to imagine what it was like having so many "brothers" and "sisters" hanging around.

"What can I say? Cathy and Pete love kids. I guess that's why they were happy to take me in."

"But eight! I mean, that's not normal."

"What's normal?" Beth stared at him. He stayed silent; he, of all people, couldn't answer that question.

"I have to share a room with Mia." She frowned. "She's a pain. Always looking through my stuff. It's hard to keep things private."

She picked up a framed photo. "Is this you with your dad?"

Jack nodded, pulling a face. He hated having his picture taken. Who'd want to be constantly reminded they resembled a slug? But Mum had sneaked up behind him as they'd walked in the woods near where they used to live. She'd called out his name and he'd turned as she snapped the photo. His expression, half-obscured by the hood of his jacket, was one of questioning surprise. It had been one of the rare times Dad had gone with them. He'd also turned towards the camera, the skin around his blue eyes crinkled as he laughed into the lens. Jack remembered how they'd ended up playing football in a field behind the woods, as the sky darkened and clouds gathered overhead. Eventually it started to rain and they'd got drenched running home. Dad had been chilled out that day – not in one of his moods. Life with Dad was like being on a roller coaster at times, with stomach-churning ups and downs.

"You look like him." She replaced the picture. "People used to say I looked like my dad." Her shoulders stiffened for a moment, before she relaxed them and sank into the battered armchair. Her black rucksack, which Jack had started to think must be superglued to her, was nestled between her feet.

He fetched glasses of juice for them both from the kitchen and set them on the floor.

"What's up?" said Beth, gazing at him with her black-rimmed eyes. "You've been itching to say something since I got here, I can tell. So . . . spit it out."

He hadn't realised it was so obvious. He told her what he'd found out about Dad. "I haven't time to wait for him to phone again in two weeks. My skin's a disaster zone."

Beth sipped her juice. "Has he always been this useless?"

He gave her a dirty look. Dad wasn't useless. Well, maybe he was a little. Whenever away for work, he'd rarely phone. But that was because he got caught up in whatever he was working on . . . wasn't it?

Beth stretched her back, flinging her arms into the air and yawning. "Perhaps he's so busy, he's forgotten about you."

Jack scowled, but a tiny part of him wondered if she had a point. What was that old saying? *Out of sight; out of mind.*

"Have you tried phoning or emailing him?"

"Look, I'm not stupid," he said, his voice rising in indignation. "He doesn't have a phone. And his email's not working. It bounces my messages back. It's like he's closed his account." He cleared his throat and swallowed. "The thing is, I'm no good at that investigating stuff. I'd like your help, if you're still offering it, that is?"

Beth grinned. "I thought you'd never ask."

"I haven't blown it then?"

"Nah, takes more than one knockback to put me off." Beth punched him lightly on the shoulder. "Right, let's get to work. We should start with your aunt. She's the one who heard from your dad last. She's bound to know what's going on. Where does she live?"

"Colford," he said, rubbing his chin. "And I remember Mum saying once that Dad used to work near there."

"So, it's a great place to start,' she said. "Have you been there before?"

"I visited her during the Christmas holidays, but—"

"Let's go there then."

"Can't we ring her? It's over three hours on the bus."

"If something's happened, she's not going to talk about it over the phone, is she? Face to face, that's the way to go, trust me," said Beth. "Come on!"

"Wait!" To Jack's astonishment Beth had grabbed her rucksack and stood waiting for him by the door. "We can't just leave. What about my mum and Cathy?"

"We'll ring them when we get there. If we wait, it might be too late for you. Would your mum let you go if you asked? Even Cathy wouldn't and she's really relaxed about me doing my own thing."

Beth was right. Mum got extra anxious about him in the summer months. Better to leave without her having the chance to say no to the trip. She was so brittle at the moment, one wrong word from him and she'd snap like a dry twig.

"Cathy's away," said Beth. "And Pete's so busy with the others he won't miss me for a while. It'll be cool – don't worry."

"There's another problem," said Jack, putting his hand on the door to stop her rushing out. "I can't travel during the day because of the sun."

"Oh." Beth plonked herself in a chair, looking dejected. She stared into space for a moment. Then she leant forwards and slapped her knees with her hands. "We'll go tonight then. Right now, we can start making a list of questions to ask her. Like proper detectives. Got any paper?"

Reluctantly, he fetched a pad of paper and a pencil. He had the feeling Beth wasn't taking his predicament seriously. "Do we need to write it down? I'm sure I'll know what to ask when I see Auntie Lil."

But she had already started jotting something on the pad in large loopy writing. Jack peered over her shoulder.

At the top she'd scribbled:

The Case of the Missing Dad

"Why did you write that? It looks stupid."

"Okay, I'll cross that bit out." Beth put a line through it and underneath wrote a short list of questions.

1. Does Auntie Lil know where your dad is?

2. Where is he?

3. How can we get hold of him?

"There are three possible explanations. Either your dad's too busy to contact you. Or, he doesn't want to see you. Or . . ." Beth raised both hands in the air and fluttered her fingers in a bad imitation of a ghost, ". . . something sinister's happened to him. Whichever's right you still need to find him urgently, correct?"

Jack shrugged. Beth was like a whirlwind, darting here and there, making snap decisions. Jack couldn't help wondering if involving her in all this was such a great plan. But he'd asked for her help and that was that. There was no going back now. And what else could he do? Sit around waiting for Dad to show up? He could be waiting a long time. And things had gone too far for that.

Chapter Seven

Pulling his ear buds out, Jack glanced at his watch: ten p.m. There had to be another half an hour before they got to Colford. Boredom settled on him like a heavy cloud, dampening his spirits further. And when bored he always got in a stew over his problems, going around in circles and never getting anywhere. He needed to distract himself, to blot out the thoughts rioting in his head.

"Er, Beth."

She looked up at him from the paperback she'd been immersed in since they'd boarded the bus.

"Why do you wear so much make-up? You'd look good without it." Somehow that hadn't come out quite right.

Beth shrugged her shoulders, folding the page corner

over and closing the book with a snap. "Are you saying I look ugly?"

"I didn't mean . . ." Jack trailed off, realising Beth was laughing at him.

"It's okay. I realise I look scary. That's the point, I suppose. It's a good way of keeping people away. Then they don't ask me questions about my mum and dad." Beth picked a fleck of grey fluff off the sleeve of her jacket and flicked it in his direction. "I don't want their sympathy anyway; I want to be left alone."

"It's doing a good job." Jack brushed the fluff off. "I nearly threw myself off the roof when I saw you. I'd do anything to blend in, but that's never going to happen."

"You're lucky." Beth yawned and stretched her back. "If you don't want to talk to someone, you just have to shake their hand . . . they'd be gone in a flash."

"Ha, ha, very funny. I've had that happen and it doesn't make me feel very lucky."

Beth chewed her lip. "Well, it's better if I'm like this, believe me."

Jack wasn't so sure, but he didn't have the chance to debate the point as Beth had shut her eyes. As she dozed off, mouth open, her head flopped onto his shoulder and a small patch of drool settled on his top near his neck. He gave up trying to push her away; the momentum of the bus always tipped her back again. Instead he closed his eyes and concentrated on thinking up a new move he could try on the roofs when they got back to the city.

He was jolted out of his thoughts by a loud thud. The bus lurched to one side. Jack seized the handle on the back of the seat in front.

Somebody screamed.

Cries of alarm shot through the bus as it veered across the road and back again. The driver braked hard, and the screech and stench of hot tyres on tarmac filled the air. Jack was thrown sideways against the window. Pain exploded in his skull. He sat dazed, clutching his head in both hands until the bus finally juddered to a stop.

There was an eerie hush for a few seconds and then everyone started talking at once. Jack stayed in his seat, too shaken to move. He touched the side of his head, grimacing; a bump had already formed under his hair. It throbbed as if shards of glass had penetrated his skull and become lodged behind his eyeballs. When he looked up he was amazed to see the glass wasn't broken or even cracked.

"Beth?" He turned to the seat beside him to find that she'd been thrown onto the floor. "Are you okay?" He stretched his hand out to help her get up.

"Yeah, I think. What's happened?" She staggered to

her feet and brushed the dirt off her clothes.

"We hit something." Jack peered out of the window, cupping his hand over his eyes to reduce the glare from the bus's internal lights. He couldn't see anything.

"I'm going to find out." Beth shuffled forwards, tripping over the bags strewn in the aisle.

With his head still throbbing, Jack stood up and scanned the luggage rack for his bag. Luckily, it had stayed put. He rummaged inside for the torch he always carried with him and followed Beth. Other passengers were checking themselves and their belongings for damage.

The driver had disappeared.

The bus door was folded open. Stepping out from the light into the night was a shock for his senses. The surrounding darkness of the countryside was total, pressing against his eyes like a black blanket. He rubbed them. Not being able to see made him kind of panicky. *Maybe this is what it's like being blind*, he thought to himself. He stood still, waiting for his eyes to grow accustomed to the gloom.

"What can you see?" asked Beth, as she sidled up to him, her warm breath tickling his neck.

"Nothing," said Jack.

"Switch this on then, you idiot." She grabbed his hand

and gave it a shake.

Jack had forgotten he was holding his torch, but as he reached for the switch, a flickering beam of light appeared from behind the bus, moving towards them.

"Don't go back there," said the bus driver as he approached them. "You'd best get back on the bus." A slight tremor in the driver's hands made the torchlight quiver.

"What's happened?" asked Beth.

"Something ran out in front of the bus," said the driver, shakily. "Not sure what it was. Nothing out there now. I'll need to radio in and report it. And we've got a puncture too." He climbed up the steps to the bus. Jack watched him inside, waving his hands around wildly while talking to one of the other passengers.

"Let's go and have a look," said Beth.

"Why do you want to do that?" Jack asked in horror.

"Oh come on. Whatever it is might not be dead; we may be able to help it. Anyway, if I want to go into medicine when I'm older, I'll need to get used to that kind of thing."

Jack looked at her in amazement. He couldn't believe she already knew what she wanted to do with her life. He hadn't given his own future much thought.

"It's why I always carry a first-aid kit," she continued.

"A good job too, travelling with you."

Jack followed half-heartedly. He really didn't want to search for a wounded animal, and he didn't share Beth's fascination with blood and injury. He had enough of his own injuries to cope with. But he wasn't about to leave her to wander off on her own in the dark, so he switched on his torch and they set off in the direction the driver had come from.

The thin shaft of light didn't illuminate much, apart from a strip of tarmac directly in front of them. No traffic passed them as they walked. The air was silent and heavy and the smell of burnt rubber still lingered. The only sounds Jack heard were the scrunch of their shoes on the road and the faint babble coming from their fellow passengers on the bus. A thin film of moisture had formed above his top lip. He wiped it off with his sleeve. The further from the bus they walked the more nervous he became. And he didn't understand why.

"We'll never find it," he said, after a minute of fruitless searching. "Let's go back."

"Wait. What's that?" Beth pointed to the side of the road a few metres away.

A lump, which from a distance looked like an old sack, lay beside the grass verge. They drew nearer.

In the pale glow of the torch's beam Jack could now

make out the body of an animal, its coat matted with blood, tongue protruding from the corner of its mouth. One of its front legs was twisted into an impossible shape, the bone poking through the surface of the skin. Jack's throat constricted as he fought a sudden queasiness. It was a dead Labrador.

He moved closer still and saw that patches of hair were missing. The bald areas were covered with red blisters. An icy chill spread through Jack's body. Okay, the dog had been run over, but something else had caused those hideous sores.

Chapter Eight

"Who would let a dog get into such a state?" Beth spat the words out in anger. "And let it out on the road?"

Jack bent to look more closely at the wounds and immediately wished he hadn't. His stomach did several somersaults and a nasty taste rose up in his mouth; he swallowed quickly and stepped away again. The torch trembled in his hand. "Why does its body have so many sores? They look like burns."

"There's a name tag." Beth stooped and gently brushed the dog's fur from around its collar. She took the torch from Jack.

"*Rex*," she said. "Wait, there's something else. A telephone number – I can barely read it – four, five, four, two, three. I think the last one's a two or a five." She stood up again. "Let's go back – this is giving me the creeps."

Jack couldn't agree more. He shivered. Something troubled him about the dog, but for the moment he couldn't quite put his finger on what it was.

"I'm afraid this bus won't be going any further, folks," the driver was saying when they returned. "The replacement will take an hour or so to get here, so you can either make yourselves comfortable and wait or make your own arrangements."

Groans came from a few of the passengers and a general hum of conversation began as people decided what to do. The driver moved through the bus, checking everyone was unharmed and answering questions.

"This is so boring," said Beth. "Do you know the way to your aunt's house from here?"

Jack nodded and then realised what Beth was getting at, "You want to walk? It's pitch-black out there."

"You've got a torch. It can't be that difficult. Is it far?"

Jack shook his head. "Well, if you're sure; but don't say I didn't warn you."

They slipped off the bus while the driver was preoccupied with a tearful old man, and they were soon jogging in the direction of Colford. After twenty minutes Jack caught sight of the lights of the town twinkling in the distance. He stopped by a sign for a public footpath.

"It's going to get tough from now on," he said. "We've got to go cross country."

"You mean this isn't tough?" panted Beth, as she staggered up to the stile where Jack stood. "I thought you said it wasn't far."

"It's not." Jack bit his lip, a snort of laughter threatening to burst from him. "It's always more difficult walking in the dark."

"It wouldn't be half as bad if you didn't keep waving that torch around instead of keeping it still. Then I'd know where to put my feet." She muttered something that sounded like "mad boy" under her breath, as she heaved herself over the stile.

A few minutes passed in silence as they concentrated on placing one foot in front of the other on the track skirting the field. The grass rustled under their feet, disturbing the stillness of the air.

A snap to his right caused Jack to stop in his tracks. Beth cannoned into him. Despite the muggy heat, a chill spread along his arms, making the little hairs stand to attention.

"Did you hear that?" he croaked. "A noise from over there." He swung his torch towards the trees. "Something's moving about . . ."

There was a cracking sound. It came from the path ahead. Beth seized the torch and pointed it along the track.

"What is it? You're spooking me out." Jack's voice wobbled. He peered into the blackness. Two shapes flitted across the path. They disappeared into the trees.

"Some kind of animal." Beth handed the torch back to him. "Chill, it's probably a deer. It's not like anything else is going to be out here, is it?"

Jack gave a nervous chuckle. Night-time noises didn't normally bother him, especially as he spent so much time traipsing around in the dark. He had to pull himself together – finding the dead dog had unnerved him. And like Beth said, only animals would be around at that time of night.

But Jack continued to feel uneasy. Every snap of a twig, every rustle in the undergrowth brought him out in a cold sweat. He wanted to get to Auntie Lil's. He quickened his pace. After half an hour he reached a gap in some tall wooden fence panels. It twisted between two houses – a tunnel of blackness. Jack stopped and swung the torch into the darkness, not sure if it was the right footpath. For the first time he realised how still the air had become. No sound apart from the swish of his sleeve against his side.

Something tickled the back of his neck. Startled, he spun round, swinging his bag up in front of his face.

"Relax, it's only me," said Beth. "You *are* jittery."

"Doing that doesn't help," he snapped, turning back and marching off down the pathway.

They walked thirty metres or so and then popped out into a cul-de-sac in a modern housing estate. A line of street lamps cast an orange glow on the ground.

"We're here." Jack gestured towards a small, cream-painted terraced house surrounded by a tidy picket fence.

"Wow!" Beth stood staring, open-mouthed.

"Er, I should have warned you." Jack gazed over Auntie Lil's immaculate front lawn. It was lit up by strings of white fairy lights looped over the branches of bushes and small trees. Scattered across the freshly mown grass was a huge collection of garden gnomes of different sizes, all with the same glassy-eyed, creepy expression on their ceramic faces. Some were fishing around a plastic fake pond, others wheeling barrows and yet more sitting on toadstools. Over fifty of them littered the tiny space. She'd added to them since Jack's last visit.

"My aunt collects them," he said, as he rang the doorbell. "She calls them her 'little friends'. And she's got names for them all too."

Jack could see Beth's shoulders shaking. "Don't laugh

when you meet Auntie Lil."

Beth gave him a puzzled glance, but there was no time to say more as the front door flew open and Auntie Lil stood on the step, dressed in a pair of pink pyjamas and rubbing her eyes. Jack had forgotten how tiny and round she was – so different from spindly Dad with his super-long limbs. It was difficult to believe she and Dad were family – the same flesh and blood. A strong waft of perfume enveloped him as she hugged him. Her messy bleached-blonde hair tickled his nose when she kissed him on the cheek. She looked rather like a gnome herself. But without the beard.

"What on earth are you doing here?" said Auntie Lil, gazing up at Jack in bewilderment.

"It's a long story." Exhaustion swept over him as he remembered the events of the past few hours.

"You'd better come in." Her gaze swooped from Jack to Beth, but she gave no sign she'd noticed Beth's wacky appearance. "And is this your girlfriend?"

"Auntie Lil." Heat whooshed up Jack's cheeks and ears. "This is Beth, my, um, friend."

"Oh, I see," she said and smiled at Beth, before ushering them into the sitting room. "Does your mum know you're here, Jack?"

He looked down at his trainers.

"Mmmm, I thought not. I'd better ring her. And what about yours?" she asked, looking at Beth.

"I left a note," said Beth quickly.

Auntie Lil shook her head in a "that won't do at all" way, and asked for Beth's home number. She then disappeared into the kitchen, murmuring something about making tea before tackling some awkward phone calls.

Jack noticed Beth had become strangely quiet. Even with the white stuff on her face, Jack could see she had gone a shade paler. Maybe it was the girlfriend thing that had upset her. He wished Auntie Lil hadn't mentioned it. A tiny part of him wondered what she thought of the idea of being his girlfriend, a thought he quashed as soon as it appeared. No way would she be interested in him.

"What's the matter?" he whispered. "Auntie Lil's okay really . . ."

"It's my rucksack," she whispered back. "In all the chaos with the accident and everything, I must have left it on the bus! We've got to go back right away."

"We can't go back now. The bus will have gone to be repaired. We'll go to the station tomorrow and ask if it's turned up. Auntie Lil will lend you things for tonight."

Beth reached out and grasped his arm.

"I've got to find my bag. Do you understand me?" she croaked. A tear escaped from her left eye and started trickling down her cheek. Her nails dug into him. Gently, he uncurled her fingers and rubbed his arm.

"Don't worry, we'll find it tomorrow. I promise." He tried to sound calm, but his heart hammered in his chest.

"I can't wait till tomorrow!" said Beth, gritting her teeth. "Where's the phone book? I'll ring the bus station."

Jack, not daring to reply, pointed to the low table by the radiator. A pile of directories lay next to the phone. Beth seized the top one and started rifling through it, sniffing loudly as she did so. Jack watched from the doorway. Beth's outburst dazed him. He could still feel the pressure of her nails on his arm and he pulled up his sleeve to take a look. Four angry crimson indentations marked his flesh but luckily she hadn't drawn blood from his flimsy skin.

"Got it." She picked up the phone and tapped in a number.

The ringing tone, which he heard even from his position by the door, punctured Jack's thoughts. He knew it was no use – no one would be there that time of night.

Beth slammed the phone down and turned away. He heard her trying to stifle her sobs as she hunted for something in her pocket, eventually finding a tissue and blowing her nose noisily.

"We'll find it tomorrow," he repeated lamely, not

knowing what else to say.

Later, he lay on the lumpy sofa in the sitting room, tossing and turning, struggling to get to sleep. A million thoughts whirred round in his head. Dad, crashed buses and dead dogs competed for attention in his sleep-deprived brain. But another niggling thought wouldn't go away: Beth's strange behaviour. Of course, losing her rucksack was annoying, but she had been beside herself with panic and dismay. What was in that bag? She had a secret and he wanted to know what it was.

Chapter Nine

He scrambled up the steep pitch, a forest of tall chimneys surrounding him on all sides. He could feel the smooth slates under his fingers. Above him, dark, roiling clouds. And then he slipped, skidding down towards the roof edge. Slowly at first and then faster and faster. He thrashed about, trying to grasp the slippery surface with his oily fingertips. A scream formed on his lips . . . he plummeted into the blackness.

"Jack!"

He prised his eyelids open. Auntie Lil's sitting room came into focus. Beth crouched next to him, hands on his shoulders.

"Wha . . . what's the matter?" he moaned, still half asleep.

"Get up. We've got to go."

His back and shoulders ached from sleeping on the sofa, and the side of his head was throbbing again from where he'd banged it on the bus window. His fingertips traced a lump the size of an egg under his hair.

"Where to?" He stretched, feeling the bones in his back crack as he did so. As Beth's gaze drifted over his bare chest, he quickly pulled the rumpled sheet up, a flush creeping across his cheeks. Why hadn't he brought something to wear in bed? Beth quickly glanced away.

"Bus station. You remember – I've got to find my rucksack."

Jack looked at his watch. "It's not even seven o'clock! Lost property won't be open yet." He peered at Beth, taking in her tousled black hair and the bags under her eyes. He was not the only one to have had trouble sleeping.

She sat back on her heels. "I don't care, I want to get going."

"Why are you bothered about your bag anyway?" he asked as, with one hand, he groped around on the floor for his top. "It's only stuff."

"That's so typical of a boy. It's got personal things in it. I bet you wouldn't like it if your things went missing."

"I guess you're right." He unfolded his cramped legs

and sat up. "But I'm starving. Let's grab something to eat first. Then we can think about how we're going to get over there."

"I'll skip breakfast," said Beth, as she left the room.

"It won't make lost property open any quicker!" Jack called after her and then shrugged. He really wanted to talk to Auntie Lil about Dad. Beth would have to wait to find her rucksack or do it by herself.

After finding his jeans and pulling on socks he went into the kitchen, expecting Beth to have gone off alone to the station. To his surprise, she was leaning against the worktop, eating some toast. Auntie Lil served up a huge mound of scrambled eggs and bacon on toast for him and he sat down and tucked in.

"Now, how come you two turned up on my doorstep in the middle of the night?" said Auntie Lil, as Jack scraped the last morsel of toast around his plate, soaking up the ketchup, and popped it in his mouth.

"Because Mum said you'd heard from Dad," said Jack.

"That's right. What's this about?"

"He's gone missing," said Beth, before Jack had a chance to open his mouth. If that was her way of trying to get him to hurry, it wasn't going to work.

"He can't have disappeared since I spoke to him two nights ago, surely?" said Auntie Lil, sounding faintly surprised.

Jack glared at Beth, who stood tapping her fingers on the worktop and pointedly glancing at the clock on the wall.

"He's not exactly missing, although we don't know where he is. Did he tell you where he's working?"

"I'm afraid I didn't ask, and Tom being Tom didn't volunteer the information. Let's hope he's happier now he's got another research post. Perhaps he'll start taking his responsibilities more seriously." Auntie Lil smiled gently at him. "You know your dad. He lives for his work – he needs it like he needs air to breathe. This new job will help him settle down again. I shouldn't worry about him; I'm sure he'll be in touch soon, Jack."

Jack wished he could be as sure about everything as Auntie Lil. "Didn't Dad used to work around here?"

"He did, yes." she said.

"Is it worth me going to speak to one of his old colleagues? They might have more info."

"But he wouldn't go back there after that terrible business."

"What terrible business?"

"Oh dear." Auntie Lil looked flustered and got up from the table with the toast rack in her hand. "I thought they'd have told you about it."

"You've got to tell me now, Auntie Lil. What terrible business?" he repeated impatiently.

Auntie Lil put the rack on the worktop and looked at him. "I don't suppose it'll do any harm you knowing. It was a long time ago. Your dad had a job at a facility called Bioscience Discoveries."

"Is it a research lab?" said Beth.

"Yes, and Tom was an eminent scientist. He worked on developing various drugs to do with . . . what was it? I've got a newspaper clipping here somewhere with the details." She poked around in one of the dresser drawers and finally brought out an envelope. She handed it to Jack. "He even won a prize. Ambitious – that's what he used to be."

Jack peered inside the envelope and fetched out a tatty piece of newspaper, yellowed with age. He glanced at the date: 18th June 1997. Two years before he was born. "Local scientist wins prestigious award" was printed in large bold letters.

He read the short article aloud: "A leading scientist at Bioscience Discoveries, Colford, has won an international award for his outstanding contribution to science over the past ten years. Dr Tom Phillips is being recognised for his research into liver disease.

"He has worked for Bioscience Discoveries for the last

two years and is now heading a group of scientists in pioneering work related to ageing. He is using his knowledge of how the liver regenerates to aid the development of a serum that will help the body rapidly create new cells to replace old and sick ones. These new cells will work to keep the body's organs young. The expectation is that, in the future, an eighty-year-old man or woman could have the body of a twenty year old.

"Of the award, company director, Mr Richard Blackstone, said, 'We are always pleased when one of our staff members wins an award. Dr Phillips is a valuable member of the team and an outstanding scientist. The Board congratulates him on his success.' Dr Tom Phillips, clearly delighted, said, 'It was a great surprise and honour to learn that I had won this award, especially for something I love doing.'"

A picture underneath the article showed a younger Dad, and another man, presumably Blackstone, dressed in a dark suit. A smiling woman was shaking Dad's hand and handing him a square-shaped box and envelope.

It may have been the poor quality of the newspaper picture, but, to Jack, Richard Blackstone resembled a toad. He was short, squat, with a square-shaped head and blotchy skin. His smirking mouth sliced across his face, splitting it into two uneven parts. Below his chin, a bulge of flesh billowed out like a kind of pouch. It looked as though his head rested on his shoulders without the support of a neck. Dad looked like a giant beanpole standing next to him.

"How cool to have a dad who's won an award," said Beth, staring at the photo. "I read about the liver in one of my science books. It's the one organ in the body which can repair itself when it's damaged. You know, it creates new cells or something like that."

"I never knew he'd won an award." Jack wondered what else he didn't know. "And he's never talked about working on an anti-ageing drug. I mean, that's huge. Why's he never mentioned it?"

Auntie Lil sighed. "All I know is that everything suddenly changed two years later. When you must have been – oh, I don't know – about five months old, your dad rang me and said he was leaving the company. By the next morning your parents had packed up and left town with you."

"Why?" asked Jack. "I mean, why did they leave?"

"There were a lot of tales around the town about experiments going wrong and your dad getting the blame. I suspect that's why he left. But I didn't get the chance to ask at the time, my dear, and I didn't hear from your mum and dad again for months. Tom's never been good at keeping in touch. And we've never been close, given the age difference."

Jack tried to remember how much older she was than Dad, but drew a blank. Auntie Lil's eyes took on a faraway look for a moment. "When he finally contacted me he didn't mention Bioscience Discoveries. I assumed he wanted to forget the whole episode, so I never brought the subject up. Since then, Tom hasn't stayed in a job or one place for long. With those nasty rumours around I imagine he found it difficult to find anyone who'd employ him."

"Why didn't Mum and Dad tell me any of this?"

"You were so young, dear, they had no reason to. Sometimes it's best to move on." Auntie Lil rose to her feet and started clearing the breakfast things into the sink.

"So, was Dad kicked out of his job because he messed up?" Jack's insides flipped over as he tried to make sense of what Auntie Lil had told him.

"Mistakes happen," she said, as she wiped her soapy hands on her apron. "But it was gossip and rumours. Who knows what really took place. Best you leave it at that."

He didn't know what to think. He knew so little about Dad's past. He'd tried asking when he was younger, but Dad had clammed up or changed the subject. Mum's angry argument words rattled around in Jack's head. What if Dad was so "unreliable", he'd made a mistake at work? If the rumours weren't true, why had Dad left Bioscience Discoveries in such a hurry? It didn't make sense.

"The best thing to do, my dear, is not to worry about it, sit tight here and wait for Tom to get in touch. I spoke to Maeve last night. Luckily, she'd been at work, so hadn't had a chance to worry about you, but she's not happy."

Jack hung his head; he hadn't given Mum much thought since he'd left yesterday evening.

"She's coming to pick you up on Saturday," Auntie Lil continued. "She wanted to come straight away, but I managed to persuade her to let you stay for a few days. I thought you might want a bit of a break. It wasn't easy to change her mind, though."

"Thanks, Auntie Lil," murmured Jack.

"And she's organised to take you back home too, Beth. Your poor guardian Peter was on the verge of calling the police when I rang him. My advice to you both is stay out of trouble till Saturday – go to the cinema or something."

"Before we do that," said Beth, as she headed for the back door, "the bus station must be open by now, so can we get going, please?"

Chapter Ten

Jack squeezed the tube and a dollop of cream splattered onto his hand. He rubbed the sticky substance into his face and worked it around the back of his neck. His skin cooled for a second as it soaked in, leaving tiny goosebumps on his flesh.

As he kneaded, he caught sight of his pale, shiny face in the mirror hanging in the porch. The red patch behind his right ear had grown bigger, and was clearly visible, spreading out over the top of his ear and into his hairline. His heart gave a sickening thud as he examined the layer of crusty old blood covering the centre of the blotch. He must have been scratching it during the night.

He grimaced as his fingers accidentally brushed over the sore, causing a piercing pain to shoot along the outside edge of his ear. Wiping the excess lotion onto the back of his hand in practised sweeps, he tried to push back the gloomy thoughts that kept popping into his head.

Jack glanced out of the front door. Auntie Lil stood by the kerb, next to her red Mini. She gave one final buff to the bonnet with a soft cloth and then stepped back to admire it. The perfect paintwork gleamed in the morning sunlight.

"Let's go!" called Beth, as she bounded out the house and settled into the front passenger seat. Jack, to his relief, climbed in the back behind Auntie Lil. At least sitting there he wouldn't be tempted to wrestle the steering wheel out of her hands.

Auntie Lil didn't know how to drive. Not really. That was what Jack thought anyway. What with the grinding gears, jerky starts and driving at about zero miles an hour, it was impossible to see how they were going to get anywhere.

Beth seemed jumpy. As he watched, she picked a dry flake of skin off her bottom lip. A drop of blood bubbled up which she quickly licked away. A muscle in her jaw twitched as she stared fixedly out the window. What was her problem? She was acting so weirdly. Uneasy feelings simmered along with the big breakfast inside his belly.

When Auntie Lil finally drew to a shuddering halt

outside the station, Beth sprang from the car without a word of thanks and vaulted up the steps.

"She's in a hurry," commented Auntie Lil. "Is she all right?"

"Um. Yes. Thanks for the lift," said Jack, awkwardly. "We'll make our own way back later."

Auntie Lil fumbled in her handbag and produced a twenty-pound note, telling Jack to go and enjoy himself.

"Cheers, Auntie Lil," said Jack as he pocketed the money, glad to have some extra cash to add to his dwindling supplies. He adjusted his hood, hopped out of the car and sprinted towards the main entrance of the bus station. The concourse hummed with the sound of engines and chatter of passengers milling around. There was no sign of Beth.

As he sauntered around, his eyes were lazily drawn to a bus which had just arrived. The passengers were clambering down the steps and picking their luggage up from where the driver was unloading it. As his eyes swept over the passengers, his heart skipped a beat. A familiar-looking grey-haired old lady scuffled down the steps.

"It can't be . . ." Surely Mum hadn't sent Mrs Roberts to keep an eye on him?

Jack started in the direction of the bus. Then he stopped. What was he doing? He was being paranoid. Of course it wasn't her. Even Mum wouldn't go so far as to send a neighbour to look after him. There was more than one grey-haired old woman in the country. Anyway, he had more important things to worry about. He turned on his heel to continue his search for Beth.

He eventually spotted a tatty handwritten poster with the words "Lost Property" on it. An arrow pointed to a nearby door, the glass panels smeared with marks and fingerprints. He pushed it open and entered a small windowless room with a row of stackable, plastic chairs lined up along the wall to his left. A single poster was stapled to a cork noticeboard with the warning "You Are Being Watched" and a drawing of a giant hand pointing out of the poster towards him. As he moved further into the room the finger seemed to follow. The back of his neck tingled. A wooden counter, with an ancient computer sitting on it, ran along the width of the room. Behind the counter, an archway led into a storage room, with shelves stacked high with bags, suitcases and other items people had left behind. Beth was standing at the counter.

"They've found it!" she said as she spotted him, her smile stretching across her face. Whatever was in the rucksack, she was very happy to get it back.

"Here you go." A man appeared from the storeroom and dumped her rucksack on the top of the counter.

"Careful!" Beth seized hold of it, glaring at the man as she did so. Jack couldn't help remembering how she'd snapped at him when he'd tried to pick her bag up. This man wasn't being treated any better.

"What have you got in there? Rocks or something?" The man muttered a few words under his breath and then grabbed a clipboard and pen. Beth scrawled her name where he pointed. He tore off the top copy and handed it to her. "Your receipt."

With the man looking on suspiciously, Beth hauled the rucksack off the counter and crouched on the floor, undoing the zip as she did so. She peeped into the small gap she'd made. Jack peered over, trying to get a glimpse of what was inside. But Beth was too quick for him. With a decisive twang, she pulled the zip shut, stood up straight and slung the bag over her shoulder.

The jittery feeling was back again, but he did his best to shrug it off. What did it matter what she kept in her bag? It was none of his business. Now she had it back, at least they could concentrate on finding Dad. All the same, he wished she'd stop being so secretive.

"Let's go to Café Manon," he said. "We can talk there."

They left the station and dashed over to the shady side of the market square beside the medieval church. On the cobbles in front of the café were three or four metal tables, already occupied by people enjoying the early morning warmth. Inside it was still cool and practically deserted. An old couple sat by the window sipping cups of tea and a bearded man read the newspaper by the counter.

Jack whipped out the twenty-pound note Auntie Lil had given him.

"I'll have an orange juice, since you're paying," said Beth, giving him a cheeky grin and taking a table near the door.

"I need to keep away from the glass," said Jack, gesturing towards the back of the café. "Reflective light."

"Oops, sorry," she said and moved tables. Jack ordered the drinks and then carried them over, setting them on the blue and white chequered plastic cloth. Beth held her rucksack on her lap. *She's scared to put it down*, thought Jack, as he pushed the vase of fake flowers out of the way.

Beth took a sip of her drink and then banged the glass down. "Right, let's get to work." She leant forwards, resting her elbows on the table. "We need to get on with investigating Bioscience Discoveries."

Jack sighed. "What's the point? Dad left fourteen years ago and Auntie Lil said he'd never go back. Where're you going?" Beth had stood up.

"Back in a sec." She went over to the counter and

started talking to the woman behind it. A minute later she returned and slid back into her seat. "According to the waitress, the best person to talk to about Bioscience Discoveries is Ted Harris. He left there years ago, so he's more likely to spill the beans." Beth reached and grasped Jack's wrist, pulling it roughly to inspect his watch. "And he should be coming in here in the next half an hour. All we have to do is wait."

She lifted her glass and slurped some juice through the straw.

It wasn't long before Beth pointed through the window at a figure on the pavement, pushing a yellow cart loaded with assorted brushes. She jumped up from her seat and was out of the door before Jack could move. He slapped his drink down and hurried after her.

"Ted Harris?" said Beth as she approached the man.

"Who's asking?" The man put a hand to his mouth and wiped his lips.

"I'm Beth. That's Jack. We've been told you used to work at Bioscience Discoveries?"

"Wha' you interested in that place for?" said Ted, looking shiftily over his shoulder. His voice was deep and grating. Up close Jack saw the dirt on his clothes, his long hair and beard matted and greasy, and his fingernails blackened with grime. When he moved a sour odour wafted past Jack's nose – the stench of someone who hadn't had a bath any time in the last month.

"Um . . ." Jack's mind went blank. No help came from Beth. Her power of speech seemed to have temporarily abandoned her. She stood with her mouth clamped firmly shut, probably to avoid inhaling the smell.

"What's in it for me, if I talk to you?" Ted rubbed a grubby finger across his lips.

"A cup of coffee," said Beth, finally finding her voice. "In the caff."

"And a bun?" The shadow of a grin appeared on the man's face. Jack caught a fleeting glimpse of stained teeth.

Beth nodded and they went back inside to their table. This time she squeezed next to Jack, leaving the other side of the table for Ted.

As soon as he had his coffee and iced bun in front of him, Ted glanced across the table at them.

"If you young 'uns know what's good for you, you'll stay well clear of that place."

"What . . . why?" asked Beth.

The man let out a short bitter laugh which turned into a hacking cough. Jack jerked his head back, but wasn't quick enough to avoid a strong whiff of the man's stale tobacco breath hitting him squarely in the face.

"I used to work there," the man said, once he had managed to clear his lungs. "A long time ago. Couldn't stand it any longer. 'Ad to leave. It's better to sweep the streets. Strange things go on there. Bad experiments. Can't say no more." Ted shuddered and glanced over his shoulder again. "They've got spies everywhere."

"Spies?" Despite himself, Jack's eyes followed the man's gaze.

"See them over there? They could be spies. Or her." He pointed at Beth. "She could be one."

"She's not a spy!" said Jack. Beth glared at the man.

"Listen." The man jabbed the table with a grubby finger as if to emphasise the point. "Spies can be anyone, like you or me. Your neighbour might be a spy, or your gran. Think about it."

"Thanks for that, we'd better get going." Beth glanced at Jack, rolling her eyes in the direction of the door.

"And that Blackstone . . ." Ted tapped a temple with his forefinger. "Power's made him crazy." He stuffed the remainder of the bun in his mouth, gulped down his coffee and got up, shuffling towards the door.

"Wait!" called Jack.

The man paused. "The papers; they'll explain it all. I gave 'em everything I 'ad."

The door banged shut as the strange man walked out.

Jack and Beth were left staring at each other, open-mouthed.

The waitress came over and started clearing the glasses away, clicking her tongue as she did so.

"Poor Ted. He comes in here every week." The waitress paused in her wiping of their table. "They accused him of giving secrets away, though what secrets Ted would have . . ." She shook her head, looking mystified. "He was a cleaner."

She bustled away and Jack and Beth sat looking at each other in stunned silence.

"Is he nuts?" asked Jack, eventually. "Or do you think he was telling the truth about Bioscience Discoveries?"

"No idea," Beth shivered. "But there's something going on at that place. First we find out your dad left there in a hurry and now Ted's warning us off. Shame we didn't have a chance to ask him if he ever met your dad."

"And what did Ted mean by 'look in the papers'? What papers?"

"The newspapers, you numbskull. There's one place we can find some answers."

"Where?"

"The library. They're bound to have a computer." She stood up and swung her rucksack over her shoulder, catching the vase with the trailing strap. Jack stretched out a hand to try and steady it. The vase teetered and then crashed to the floor, shattering into tiny fragments.

The waitress hurried over with a dustpan and brush as Beth, face beetroot with embarrassment, scuttled around picking up stray pieces.

"There you go." The waitress gave a final sweep and sped off to deposit the shards of glass in the rubbish bin. She returned with a new vase and carefully replaced the artificial flowers.

"Let's get out of here, before I do any more damage," said Beth, her face still pink.

"Wait a sec," said Jack. He couldn't hold his curiosity in any longer. "What's with you and that bag? What have you got in there? A horde of stolen money? A headless corpse? What?"

"It's nothing." Beth clutched the rucksack tightly.

"Look." He was getting irritated with Beth for acting so mysteriously. "We need to clear this up, right? I've trusted you with a lot of stuff about me and my family. You should know by now if you can trust me or not. If you don't, maybe you should go back home straightaway. Because I don't want to hang around with someone who keeps secrets."

A long pause followed. He started to wish he hadn't said anything. Now he was worried he'd upset her. He licked his lips nervously and took a swig of juice. All the time he was aware of Beth's gaze on him, as if she was weighing something up in her mind.

After what seemed like an eternity, she sat back down and hauled the rucksack onto the table. She undid the zip. Slowly she lifted two wooden boxes out and placed them in front of him.

The boxes were identical: each one roughly the same size as a large box of teabags. They were made from a cheap-looking, light-coloured wood and covered with crude carvings of leaves and flowers. They looked, to Jack, like they'd been knocked up in somebody's shed. A brass plaque was screwed to the front of each.

Gingerly, he picked one of them up and almost dropped it. It was heavy.

"Don't!" said Beth, snatching the box from him and placing it back on the table. The waitress looked over at them.

"They're precious to me," hissed Beth. "I don't want them damaged."

"What are they?"

She fumbled with the clasp of one of the boxes and opened the hinged lid. It flipped back onto the tablecloth with a soft rap. Jack craned forwards to peer inside.

"What the . . . ?"

81

Chapter Eleven

All Jack could see was a large heap of fine, greyish dust lying on a purple lining.

"Don't breathe," said Beth. "Or it'll blow away."

"What is it?"

"Ashes."

"Ashes?"

"My parents' ashes."

"What?" Jack sat back quickly. He'd never seen a dead person's ashes before. It wasn't the kind of thing he expected someone to carry around with them in a rucksack.

"Jack, meet Mum and Dad." Beth snapped the lid shut and pointed in turn to each of the boxes. He noticed that names were inscribed on the metal plaques: "Rosie

Sullivan" and "Paul Sullivan". Underneath each of the names was the simple phrase, "Beloved parent of Beth".

"Shouldn't . . . I mean . . . shouldn't they be in a churchyard . . . or crematorium, or something?" Jack's tongue seemed to have swollen to twice its normal size and had trouble fitting in his mouth. At the same time his brain creaked into action, as he tried to remember what Mum had done with his grandmother's ashes when she'd died.

"Maybe, but I couldn't decide where Mum and Dad would want to be. I'm searching for the best spot to scatter them."

"And you've carried them around with you all this time?"

"Yup, for two years. I like to have them near me."

"They're heavy," he said. "I mean the ashes. They're heavier than I'd have thought, you know, a dead person . . . How do you manage to carry them all the time?"

Beth regarded him, he could have sworn, with something close to pity. "You get used to it."

Jack was stunned. What did you say to someone who'd lost both their parents at once in a tragic accident and then lugged the remains around in a rucksack? It didn't sound as if Beth was as over their deaths as she'd tried to make out. But then again, what did he know? He'd never lost anyone. Apart from his grandparents and he hadn't been very close to them. Perhaps if his parents died he would do exactly the same thing.

"You think I'm mad, don't you?" Beth closed the lid and stroked her hand across the top of the box.

"No, no." Jack scoured his brain for words to describe what he was feeling. "It's just not what I expected. To be honest, I'm relieved. After what I've been imagining, carrying your dead parents' ashes around with you . . . isn't that bad." The last remark came out in a kind of high-pitched squeak.

"I don't usually tell people what's in the bag, in case they freak out."

At least he'd managed not to do that.

He watched as Beth struggled to put the hefty makeshift urns back in the bag and then zipped it up again. "I did think you were mad last night."

"Yes, sorry. I was upset," Beth admitted, smiling. "Anyway, I'm glad I've shown you and I've got no more secrets now, I promise."

"When will you know you've found the right spot . . ." Jack gestured towards the bag, ". . . to scatter them?"

"I'll know it when I see it," said Beth, as she got to her feet again. "Come on. We've got some investigating to do at the library."

Jack stood up quickly, the ever-present itch on his hand a reminder of why they were there. The problem was, more and more pieces were being added to the puzzle, but none of them fitted together. Nothing made sense.

Then something clicked in his brain. Something Ted had said. What was it? About spies. *They've got spies everywhere. Your neighbour* . . . Jack stopped abruptly by the café door. Mrs Roberts. She was always snooping. Could it really have been her at the bus station? Was it possible she was a spy? He almost laughed out loud at the thought. And yet . . .

Beth nudged him. "Come on. Let's go."

He gave himself a little shake. He had to snap out of this or he'd be getting suspicious of everyone and everything. He'd speak to Beth later about the whole spy thing. For the moment, he had to focus on looking for Dad and at least keeping busy meant he wasn't dwelling so much on his worsening skin.

There were so many unanswered questions. He wondered how anything Ted had told them could lead to Dad. But it was the one clue they had and he couldn't think of what else to do.

Chapter Twelve

Jack lifted his hood as they left the café. He flitted between the shadows of the shops and buildings. Beth strode along beside him. They made their way to the corner of the market square. That's when he saw her. The same stooped figure, with a wisp of grey hair that he'd seen at the station. She disappeared round the side of a shop. The woman looked so much like Mrs Roberts it could have been her double. But if it really was her, what *was* she doing there?

"What's up?" said Beth.

"I thought I saw someone I know."

"Come on," she said, glancing down the street. "I want to get to the library."

Jack hesitated. "You go on ahead. The library's on the

street to the right. I'll meet you there."

"What are you going to do?" Beth turned to stare at him and raised her eyebrows.

"I've got to check something." He sprinted off down the street before Beth could complain. This was something he needed to do by himself. He didn't want to scare Mrs Roberts – just find out why she was there.

He hurried to the corner and peered round in time to see the hunched figure shuffle into a narrow, fenced alleyway. He dithered for a moment at the entrance and looked up at the sky. Clouds littered the expanse of blue, blocking the sun from sight for now. But it wouldn't last long. Whatever he decided to do, he'd have to be quick. His skin would cook if he stayed outside.

He didn't like the idea of becoming a sinister stalker. Say it wasn't her? He'd be tailing an innocent old lady round the town. On the other hand, Ted from the café had spooked him with all his talk of spies. What if she was spying on him?

Decision made.

Luckily, overgrown trees in the bordering gardens provided patches of deep shade on the narrow path. A slight breeze rustled and scratched the leaves against the fencing, and shadows cast gloomy shapes on the panels and ground in front of him. About thirty metres away,

Jack could see Mrs Roberts. She scurried along, taking small quick steps. He picked up his pace. He didn't want to lose sight of her, but he also didn't want her to turn round and spot him. Not until he knew where she was going.

The path veered a little to the right, running behind a terrace of Victorian houses. He recognised the distinctive roof tiles and chimney pots peeping between the trees. The old lady stopped. Jack ducked under some branches, flattening himself against the fence. He hoped the leaves would hide him. Peeping through the twigs, he was in time to observe her open a slatted gate and disappear through it.

As soon as she'd gone, he sped after her. Finally he reached the spot where she'd disappeared. There were two gates immediately in front of him and another a little further along.

"Which one?" he said to himself.

In the end he plumped for the middle gate which he was pretty sure she had used. He twisted the ring handle and pushed. Locked.

He glanced up and down the path – no one in sight. Then he examined the gate, flexing his fingers. He could imagine Beth rolling her eyes at him and saying, "It's not a roof, Jack."

Being able to jump and climb had its uses on the ground too, though. He stretched up and grasped the rough wood at the top. He lifted his left foot onto one of the struts and pushed upwards so that he ended up straddling the gate. Below him was an overgrown garden with knee-high weeds and unkempt bushes scattered amongst tall grass. An old magnolia tree obscured his view of most of the house. Gnarled, low-hanging branches almost met the ground and goblet-shaped pink flowers clung between the leaves. Carefully, he lowered his body down, hoping nobody had spotted him. He crept towards the house, skirting round the edge of the garden where the foliage was thickest.

Squatting underneath one of the windows, he raised his head so he could see over the sill. The room was empty. He huffed in frustration. She might have gone into the front room. There was no hope of getting round there; he'd already noted that there was no side gate.

Maybe she's gone upstairs, he thought to himself.

He glanced at his watch. He needed to act fast. An itchiness was beginning to spread across his cheeks, a sign his skin was reacting to the sun's rays. On impulse, Jack grabbed a low limb of the nearby magnolia and swung himself into it. The numerous thick branches provided a choice of footholds. He scrambled up until he was level with the upstairs window. Scooting on his backside along a large branch, one leg either side, he edged towards the glass pane. He peeped in.

There was a bed in the room pushed against the left wall, and on the right was a dressing table. A pair of pink slippers lay by a chest of drawers.

Leaves from the branch crackled and grated against the glass. The noise seemed magnified to his ears. His heart beating rapidly, he scooted backwards. Grabbing the nearest branch he started to lower himself to the ground. As he reached one of the last boughs, there was a loud crack. He yelled in alarm as he crashed through the leaves, hitting the grass with a thud. He lay there winded, ribs aching as if he'd been punched.

He lurched to his feet and stumbled back through the garden. Every bone in his back throbbed. As he heaved himself over the gate, he looked back. A figure stood at the window staring out at the garden. An old lady with grey hair and a hunch. It had to be Mrs Roberts – who else could it be?

Jack dropped into the alley and kicked the fence in frustration. His skin felt fiery hot – he'd been out in the sun long enough. Confronting Mrs Roberts would have to wait to another day.

He hobbled to the library and found Beth waiting for

him outside.

"What's wrong?" she asked.

"I thought . . ."

"What?" Beth scrunched her black eyebrows together into a puzzled frown.

They've got spies everywhere . . . Ted's words hung in his mind. Beth would think he'd gone mad. He shrugged. "Oh nothing. I'm imagining things."

Chapter Thirteen

Jack tried to banish the prickle of worry he had about Mrs Roberts, as he led the way through the revolving door of the library. A ceiling fan whirred feebly above them. The air hung heavily with the smell of musty books and the lonely rustle of pages from an old newspaper lying discarded on a table under the fan. The library was deserted, apart from Mr Parrot.

"Hi, Mr Parrot." Jack approached the elderly librarian, standing at the front desk, stacking books into a pile. A pair of glasses were perched on top of his silver-grey hair. He looked up and smiled warmly when he saw Jack.

"Hello. Jack, isn't it? Good to see you again." He paused in his book sorting. "How long's it been since your last visit? It must be six months at least."

"'Bout that." Jack remembered the hours he'd spent in the library when he'd visited Auntie Lil over the Christmas holidays. He'd played computer games because it was too bright for him to be outside.

"What can I do for you?" Mr Parrot asked.

He explained what they wanted and the librarian led the way to the computer in the corner of the reference section.

"You can do a general search on the internet, if you wish, but you might find the most useful information collected in our 'NewsStore' database. Did you use it on your last visit, Jack? Many of the local and national papers, from 1995 up till now, have been downloaded onto the system. But there are a lot of pages. Are you looking for something in particular?"

"Anything to do with Bioscience Discoveries from 1999 onwards."

"1999." Mr Parrot adeptly clicked the computer mouse with his wizened finger to find the file. "Here we are. This is the local newspaper, *The Colford Echo*, and the right year. If you need any help, please ask. Though you youngsters are good at this sort of thing." He gave a wheezy chuckle and moved away.

"Thanks." Jack sat at the computer while Beth pulled up a spare chair.

He typed "Bioscience Discoveries" into the search box and hit return. A few seconds later the titles of hundreds of articles appeared in a list.

"Type in 'experiments' as well," said Beth. "It might shorten it."

Jack hit return again. They waited. Again a long list popped up.

"What about using Blackstone's name?"

That didn't make much difference; the new list that popped up still contained hundreds of entries. "We don't have enough information to narrow it down." Jack drummed his fingertips on the desk in frustration.

Beth puffed out her cheeks, a frown line appearing between her eyebrows. "We'll have to go through them one by one."

Jack clicked on the first entry and they started reading.

Ten minutes later and they had hardly made a dent in the records.

"I'm seeing double," moaned Beth.

"We'll have a break soon." Jack was starting to feel dejected. The initial excitement at the prospect of finding some useful information had worn off. He was beginning to think they weren't going to discover anything interesting to do with Bioscience Discoveries.

"Stop! Go back!" Beth waggled her hands in front of

the screen.

Jack clicked the back button and straightaway saw what had caught Beth's eye. It was dated 18th November, 1999. He read it aloud. "'Child Experimentation Horror at Local Labs. A former employee of Bioscience Discoveries has contacted our newspaper claiming he has information that experiments on children are taking place at the lab. Our informant, who wishes to remain anonymous, told us: "Dr Tom Phillips and his team are testing anti-ageing drugs on babies as young as a few months old. I've seen procedures being carried out both on animals and children at the research facility. The side effects these children suffer are horrific – some have blisters the size of my fist on their tiny bodies." Our informant has contacted the police with his claims and a police spokeswoman has told us these are being investigated. We'll keep you posted with all the developments.'"

Jack went hot, sweat prickling his scalp. He sat back in his chair, his mouth opening and closing like a fish, but no words came out. He looked at Beth in disbelief.

"Child experimentation!" she exclaimed. "So that's what Ted was hinting at! He must have been the newspaper's informant. The whole thing sounds like something out of a sci-fi film."

Jack leant forwards, clicking the mouse repeatedly and staring at the articles flashing up on the screen. "Dad would never do anything like that. It can't be true." His voice sounded shaky to his ears.

"There must be other stuff to do with your dad leaving the company," said Beth.

After sifting through two or three more pages, they found another article. This one couldn't be missed: "Blackstone's Bioscience Lab in Crisis!" screamed the large headline, this time from the front page of *The Colford Echo*. The date: 21st December, 1999.

"'Rumours are rife concerning the future of Bioscience Discoveries,'" read Jack aloud, "'as company director Richard Blackstone yesterday announced the surprise departure of leading scientist Dr Tom Phillips. Dr Blackstone stated that Dr Phillips wished to spend more time with his family. The shock announcement comes amidst claims made to this newspaper, by a former employee of Bioscience Discoveries, that scientists at the laboratory are involved in experimenting on children. Asked if Dr Phillips's leaving had anything to do with child experimentation, Blackstone issued the following statement:

"'"We at Bioscience Discoveries have a long and proud history of providing safe and effective treatments for a range of disorders and diseases which affect the human population. These rumours are totally unfounded. Our aim is to cure, not to harm. We will continue to do so, working with our highly qualified scientists. Dr Phillips's departure is a disappointment but we wish him well for the future." Dr Phillips was unavailable for comment.'"

After scanning a few more articles they hit on another short piece: "Police are closing the file on Bioscience Discoveries, a spokeswoman confirmed today, citing lack of evidence to back up the claims of wrongful experimentation as the reason."

So many questions buzzed around in Jack's brain, it ached, the horror of what they'd read hitting him like a punch to the heart. And a tiny, niggling voice in his head kept worrying at him. All this was more serious than the mistakes Auntie Lil had spoken about. Could Dad have been involved in horrifying experiments on children? Did the company find out and tell him to leave? Maybe that was why he'd had so many problems keeping a job. Jack wanted to believe he was innocent. He couldn't imagine his award-winning dad could be capable of *that*. But something didn't add up. What did he really know about Dad? He'd spent more time at work than at home – Jack had hardly seen him even before he and Mum split up. When he did, he was grumpy. And much of Dad's past was still a mystery. What if all the stuff in the newspapers was true?

He scratched his plastered hand and caught Beth staring at him with an anxious look on her face.

"I know what you're thinking," she said. "But it was only rumours about the experimentation. The police didn't find anything. Perhaps he left because he really did want to be with you more."

"But why leave so suddenly?" said Jack, at last managing to get his voice to work. "And stating he wants to spend more time with his family – it's another way of saying he's been fired, isn't it? There's so much I don't understand." Jack thumped the keyboard with his fist, causing Mr Parrot to glance over at them from his desk. "But I know one thing: he ran away – isn't that what a guilty man would do?"

Chapter Fourteen

Outside the library, Jack jabbed a hand in his pocket to find money for a taxi.

"If Dad's been involved in some sort of sick experimentation on children, there's no point looking for him any more. He's not going to be interested in helping me. He's probably working on some equally horrible scientific project right this minute."

"You're overreacting," said Beth. "It's the shock of reading all the stuff in the library. Don't believe everything you read in the papers."

"How would you like it if your dad had been accused of experimenting on kids?" he retorted.

"You're lucky to still have a dad." Her voice sounded strained as she clambered into the taxi to go back to

Auntie Lil's. "You shouldn't give up on him so easily."

When they reached the house, Beth slammed the car door and stormed upstairs, hauling her rucksack with her. Jack trudged into the sitting room, guilt seeping out of every pore. He hadn't meant to upset Beth. To be honest, he was so wrapped up in his own problems he'd forgotten she didn't have any parents to worry about. He wondered whether he should go up and apologise, but in the end thought it'd be better to leave her alone.

Things had gone from bad to worse. He was no nearer to finding Dad. All he'd done was rake up the past and find out nasty stuff. And now he'd dug it up, he couldn't bury it again. And he'd upset his one friend. There – he'd called her his friend. Jack realised that was exactly what she'd become. Over the last twenty-four hours he had grown used to having her around and she seemed to like him. Or she had done until he'd upset her.

He sighed and looked at his watch: ten fifteen. Mum would be on her break now. He picked up the phone and rang the supermarket.

He expected an angry tirade from Mum, but she sounded more tearful and weary than anything. That made him feel worse. After he'd said sorry a million times and explained he'd been going "mad cooped up in the flat" and he "needed a break", she made him promise never to go off again without telling her. Then she calmed down and asked how he was doing now.

"Oh, fine." He stifled a pang of guilt. He hated lying to her, but what could he say? The bus had crashed into a dog, his skin was disintegrating and he'd had a fight with Beth. Oh, and Dad was a mad scientist. Mum would order him home – anxious he'd get hurt by what he'd found out, concerned his fragile skin was getting worse. No, best to grit his teeth and say nothing.

"Have you seen Mrs Roberts?" he said. Even Mum would have to admit that shadowing him to a different town, 140 miles away, was beyond the duties of a childminder.

"Mrs Roberts? Why do you ask?"

"No reason," he said. "Just thought I saw her here."

"She asked after you this morning, as I was leaving for work. She wondered where you were."

"Did you tell her?"

"Of course," said Mum in a surprised tone. "She's concerned about you. Maybe she likes your company during the day."

Jack took a sharp breath in. Mrs Roberts knew he was in Colford. He did a quick calculation in his head. She could have taken the early bus and arrived in time for him to see her at the station. He remembered what Ted had

101

said about spies and shivered.

"Has Dad called?" he asked, deciding a change of subject would be a good idea.

"Sorry, Jack, no he hasn't. Listen, love." There was a pause at the other end of the line. "You know what I was telling you the other day about me and your dad? I'm going to see the solicitor tomorrow."

"What for?"

"To formalise things – the separation."

"You said you were going to sort things out between you." Jack's voice had risen a fraction.

"Yes, and I am. Like I told you before, I've done a lot of thinking while he's been away – four months is a long time. And well . . . things weren't brilliant before he left. I don't think I can live with him any more."

Jack gripped the phone tightly. A lump had formed in his throat and his eyes began to sting – he willed himself not to cry. Had she told him? He cast his mind back to the day before he left, replaying snippets of the conversation they'd had. He couldn't remember what she'd said – the truth was he hadn't been listening.

"We'll have a proper talk in a few days, when I see you. I wanted to make sure you were clear . . ."

"Okay."

"Jack . . . I promise we'll talk more . . ."

"Yeah."

He said a choked goodbye and put the phone down. He couldn't bear to hear the concern in Mum's voice. He didn't want to listen to what she had to say. Block it out – that was the best thing to do. Concentrate on finding Dad and then everything would be all right.

He scratched his left shin. Feeling a warm stickiness beneath his hand, he peered down. A dark, damp streak had appeared on the fabric of his trousers where he'd rubbed it. His eyes widened as he stared at the stain spreading in a vertical line down his leg, and icy goosebumps rippled along his arms. He glanced at his fingers, expecting them to be covered in blood, but there was nothing to see. He knew he should roll up his jeans and take a look, but he couldn't bring himself to do it. Instead, he sat with his leg stretched out in front of him, trying to ignore the pulsing ache that radiated down his shin.

Beth came thumping down the stairs half an hour later. She strode into the sitting room, glared at him, picked up her *Junior Medical Monthly* magazine and started leafing through it.

The silence grew longer and more uncomfortable. Beth flicked through the pages, the rustling becoming louder. At last Jack couldn't take it any longer.

"Um, sorry about before."

No response. He took a deep breath. "Beth, I'm really sorry I was such an idiot."

Beth flung the magazine to one side, rushed over and threw her arms round him. "It's okay."

His body stiffened for a beat and then he allowed himself to relax into her hug, his nose buried in her hair. It smelt of flowers. He raised his arms and gently placed them around her waist and squeezed. No girl had hugged him before. Ever. It felt good.

"Thanks," he mumbled. Then, worried she'd get smeared with revolting oil, he pulled away. His face burning with embarrassment, he picked up her magazine. "What're you reading?"

"Oh, nothing. Boring stuff." She prised it from his hands, not looking at him, and placed it face down on the coffee table. Two circles of pale pink had appeared on her chalky white cheeks. He was about to ask her what the matter was when she picked up one of the telephone directories and started rifling through the pages.

"We should ring this Bioscience Discoveries place and find out if we can meet Blackstone . . . Bath Supplies, Bedroom Bargains, Bins Brickwork. Here we are. Bioscience Discoveries – four, five, four, two, three, two." Beth punched the numbers into the phone.

Jack slumped on the sofa, leant back and closed his eyes. A dull ache had started behind his right eye. Perhaps he had overreacted about the whole child experimentation thing. After all, it was ludicrous to think that Dad, who'd spent months developing a special suncream for him, would hurt anyone . . . wasn't it? There was no proof he'd been involved and the newspapers were always getting things wrong. There must be another explanation – some reason for him leaving the company. And, whatever was going on, Jack still needed to find him; that hadn't changed.

If only he could switch his brain off from thinking about all the stuff they'd found out so far – about Dad's past life, Bioscience Discoveries and that dead Labrador. Jack's eyes snapped open. The dog.

"Thanks for nothing," said Beth, slamming the phone down so hard the table shook. "The silly receptionist refused to let me speak to Dr Blackstone. She said he was too busy. Some people!"

"Never mind that now," he said. "What was the telephone number on the dead Labrador's collar?"

"Four, five, four, something," said Beth, wrinkling her forehead.

"And what's the number of Bioscience Discoveries?"

"Oh! I get you. You reckon it's the same number? But

why would a research facility have a Lab?" Beth sniggered.

"Ha ha, very funny. But it is weird."

"All the more reason for us to pay them a visit. It's useless trying to get any information on the phone. We may be able to talk to someone else who knew your dad." Beth paced the room. "But, actually, if there's something shifty going on there, like Ted said, and we turn up asking for information, we won't get anywhere."

"So what do you suggest?" asked Jack, as he gingerly flexed his left foot.

"I'll think of something on the way there. Now, are you coming or what?"

That was the difference between him and Beth, Jack thought. He always came up with the problems, what could go wrong. Whereas Beth bounded along assuming everything would turn out right. He shifted on the sofa and then moaned as a sharp pain rippled up his leg. He sank back against the cushions. "I think I need to get this sorted first."

Jack rolled up his trouser leg and Beth gasped. When he looked down he saw what she'd found so shocking. The skin below his knee had split almost right the way down the shin to his ankle. There was a thin red line of exposed flesh, with yellow pus seeping from the open wound.

Jack inspected the gash, a sick sensation bubbling up from the pit of his stomach. How had his skin got so bad so fast?

Beth reached into her rucksack and extracted her emergency first-aid kit. "I'm surprised you've been able to walk. It looks disgusting."

"What if we don't find my dad?" he said in a small voice.

"We'll find him," said Beth, firmly. "But let's deal with your leg first."

Chapter Fifteen

Jack thought it best not to tell Auntie Lil about his wound. He was convinced she'd send him home immediately and he wasn't ready for that. So he'd asked her to drop them off in town, saying they were going to the cinema. Instead they'd visited a chemist and bought antiseptic cream, painkillers and a bottle of water.

Standing now at the bus stop outside the library, Jack glanced at his watch. Half past four and still hot and sunny. The bus to Bioscience Discoveries was due any minute. He made for the shade of the doorway to wait, pulling his hood further over to shield his face. He slurped water from the bottle and popped two tablets out of the pack. After swallowing them, he sneaked his stick of lip balm out and, turning towards the wall, furtively swiped it once over his lips. Two girls came out of the library, sniggering and whispering to each other, cupped hands to mouths. Hunching his shoulders, he turned away, swiftly dropping the balm back into his pocket.

"What're you staring at, losers?" shouted Beth from the bus shelter. Her make-up had started to run, patches of pinker skin visible beneath the white. It made her look even scarier than normal.

The smaller of the girls went crimson and, muttering to her companion, they marched off down the street, glancing back every now and then. Jack slouched over to where Beth stood.

"You didn't need to call out after those girls. I can take care of myself."

"Nobody said you couldn't." She stuck out a hand. "Bus's coming."

Still feeling put out by Beth's interference, Jack stepped onto the bus. As he delved into his pocket for some change to pay the driver, Jack felt a scrunched-up paper ball in his pocket. He found a seat and fetched it out, flattening it on his knee. It was a photo. He gazed at the picture, his mind a blank. Then he remembered the thick, crumpled paper he'd plucked from the roof guttering. He'd forgotten all about shoving it in his pocket.

The picture, taken on a beach, was of a girl with a curtain of long, dark hair cascading over her shoulders. It took him a few seconds to realise the girl was Beth. She was wearing shorts and a pink T-shirt. The words "Pretty Kitty" were emblazoned across the front of it, along with the image of a black cat with pink bow around its neck. The girl sat cross-legged, on a red and black chequered picnic rug, with a man and woman kneeling behind her. The man, dark hair curling over his brow, beamed into the camera. He had one arm slung casually around the neck of the fair-haired, freckly woman. She had a pink rosebud pinned in her hair. In the background was a thick blue line of sea. Grey pebbles and sand surrounded the little group and had trickled onto the rug.

Suddenly the picture was snatched out of his hand.

"That's mine," said Beth, sharply. "Where did you find it?"

"It was on the roof. I didn't realise what it was. Are they your parents?"

Beth nodded, clutching the print to her chest and attempting to flatten the creases with her other hand. "It was taken at Witcombe Beach before they died. The last family trip we went on together. I can't believe you had it all this time. I thought it was lost forever." She gnawed her cheek, turning away from him.

Jack sat in silence, the right words refusing to form on his lips. Beth clearly didn't want to talk any more. And who could blame her? As the silence lengthened he thought about the photo. It showed a different Beth to the one who sat beside him – a happier, laughing Beth. In the picture she wasn't wearing any make-up, her face lit up by the light bouncing off the sand. She looked great. He'd never tell her that, though – he was far too embarrassed. Instead he looked out of the window at the bland landscape rolling past.

They passed field after flat field of wheat ready for harvest, the odd farmhouse and large empty barns. The road was long and straight and the chugging rhythm of the bus made Jack drowsy.

A sharp prod in his ribs woke him. He rubbed his eyes and glanced through the window in time to see the "Welcome to Selchester" sign. A drab, grey town slipped into view. Concrete office blocks and mile after mile of identical houses marked the outskirts of the town. These gave way to a street lined with small, dingy shops. The bus stopped a couple of times to let passengers on and then took a right turn signposted to "Bioscience Discoveries".

They didn't stop again until they arrived at a large site surrounded by a high chain-link fence topped with barbed wire. Inside there was an expanse of sun-scorched grass, criss-crossed by concrete pathways. Cameras on tall posts were dotted around the site. A jumble of buildings, older red-bricked three-storey ones with flat or gently sloping roofs squatted next to tall newer glass and steel constructions. A series of covered walkways and corridors, with massive floor-to-ceiling windows, linked old and new together. People scurried to and fro like giant ants.

Jack and Beth watched as everyone got off the bus. A man in uniform threw open the gate, waving each worker through as they showed him a pass. Jack then went and spoke to the driver, and learnt that the next bus would arrive in half an hour. He returned to Beth. "Let's get off and see what we can find out. We'll have to be quick – there's not much shade around here."

They hopped off the bus and walked over to the gate. The workers had vanished into the buildings. The guard came out of the gatehouse and stood in front of them, arms crossed and feet apart. His shirtsleeves were rolled up to the elbows, revealing a mass of tattoos rippling over muscled forearms. A name badge pinned to his shirt said "Neville".

"What do you want?" He looked at them, dark eyes narrowed to slits.

Jack swallowed and licked his dry lips, wishing he'd used more lip balm. "Um . . . we're here to see Dr Blackstone."

"Have you got an appointment?"

"Appointment?" Jack looked at Beth. He should have left the talking to her.

"We don't," Beth chipped in. "But I'm sure he'd want to help us with our science project for school, being in charge of such a community-spirited organisation. We wondered if we could have a look around."

The guard grunted and his bushy eyebrows knitted together in a scowl, but at least he didn't tell them to get lost.

"Wait here," he ordered. He returned to the gatehouse and picked up the phone. He left the door ajar so Jack was able to hear the conversation.

"Fiona, two youngsters have turned up saying something about a school project and wanting a tour."

Beth grinned at Jack.

"Right, you two." The guard came back out. "Looks as though you're in luck. Our Public Relations Manager is on-site today and is willing to show you around. It'll be brief, mind. She's got a meeting at five-thirty."

"Oh, thanks so, so much!" said Beth, laying it on a bit thick, Jack thought.

The guard made another quick call and another man in uniform arrived. He stayed in the gatehouse as Neville took them outside.

He silently motioned for them to follow him and they passed through the gate into the compound. The trees lining the driveway were spindly, their leaves not providing the canopy of shade Jack needed. He hugged the edge of the driveway, hopping from one shadow to another. He caught Neville casting suspicious sidelong glances at him. Beth chatted non-stop as they marched along, Neville grunting in response. To the right another security guard patrolled the perimeter fence, a large dog by his side. Jack squinted – it didn't look like a Labrador, more like an Alsatian.

Still not saying a word, Neville hurried them along the short drive towards the main entrance – a tall, imposing structure made mostly of glass and with two huge columns rising on either side of a pair of gleaming sliding doors. These swished open to reveal a massive, airy vestibule. Neville gestured for them to enter and then, without a word, disappeared back the way they'd come. Inside, it was cool – a relief from the intense heat outside. A tall blonde woman, wearing the highest heels Jack had ever seen and a dark blue skirt and jacket, stood by the polished reception desk. When she noticed them she hurried over, her heels tapping on the shiny, tiled floor. She gave them a tight-lipped smile.

"I'm Fiona Reece, Public Relations Manager. And you are . . . ?

"Beth, and this is Jack."

"So what do you want, exactly?" She switched her cool gaze between the two of them.

"We're doing a science project over the summer holidays, looking at research companies and describing what they do," Beth promptly said. She was good, thought Jack, really good.

"Which school do you go to?"

"Oh, we're on holiday," said Beth, breezily. "We're not from round here."

"Hmm." Fiona's icy stare seemed to pierce right through Jack and he lowered his eyes. Could she tell Beth was lying? "It would have been better if you'd made an appointment rather than dropping in. But I can spare ten minutes or so."

She opened a book on the reception desk and pointed to the page. "All visitors have to fill this in with their contact details."

They scribbled their names down, along with Auntie Lil's address. Fiona handed them two visitors' passes which she told them to wear at all times, then, picking up a couple of pamphlets, gestured for them to follow her.

"This leaflet is what we usually give to school parties and so on when they visit. It should give you a lot of the information you'll need for your project. I'll give you a quick tour but not many areas are open to visitors." As she said this they approached a door at the far end of the vestibule. She lifted up the pass that hung around her neck, inserted it in a keypad next to the door and punched in some numbers. There was a soft beep and a click and she pushed the door open, signalling for them to follow. They found themselves in a bright, wide corridor.

Jack noticed a security camera attached to the ceiling. As they walked along it swivelled round, tracking their movement. The hairs on his neck prickled up, a wave of unease sweeping through him at the thought of being watched.

Windows lined one side of the corridor, looking not to the outside but into a large laboratory. Inside, staff members, wearing white lab coats and masks, were busy working at benches, staring through microscopes or using pipettes with gloved hands to fill test tubes. Gleaming pieces of equipment and machinery filled the large room; everything looked white and clean. On the opposite wall of the corridor there was a series of posters in silver-grey frames. "Youth is not skin deep" proclaimed one.

"What's that mean?" asked Jack.

"Oh, that's from when the company was involved in research into anti-ageing serums. It was part of a campaign used to gain funding."

"Doesn't the company work on anti-aging stuff any more?"

"I'm not sure what happened there," said Fiona, hurrying further along the corridor. "It was before my time, but I imagine they had to stop the research for financial reasons."

"Wasn't there a scandal to do with the research?" asked Beth as she winked at Jack.

"Not that I'm aware of," Fiona replied frostily as she stopped at a window. "Now, the new building was constructed two years ago. In here we're doing our most advanced research."

"What is it about?" asked Jack.

"Mostly looking into diseases of the liver and heart conditions. In this lab, we are working on finding a cure for heart disease – to find a way to repair damaged hearts. If we could do that, we could reduce the need for transplants."

"Can we go in?" asked Beth.

"Sorry, no one's allowed in except the scientists. We need to keep conditions sterile."

Fiona moved further along the corridor, through another locked door and up a flight of stairs. She paused here and there to point out yet more labs and to tell them about the research being carried out. Jack switched off; there was only so much scientific talk he could take.

"Do you do tests on animals?" Something in the way Beth said this made Jack jump to attention. What was she playing at?

"Of course," said Fiona smoothly. "You'll find all research labs do. But we keep it to a minimum. Not many animals are used here at all. We're not one of those big animal-testing facilities."

"Can we see the test animals?"

"I'm afraid not. We limit access to those areas so as not to cause the animals unnecessary distress."

"What about . . . ?" Beth was interrupted by a loud beeping.

"Excuse me." Fiona moved over to a phone mounted on the wall.

Jack nudged Beth with his elbow. He knew she'd been going to ask about the child experimentation rumours. He had a feeling Fiona wouldn't have hesitated in chucking them out if she had. And he didn't want that to happen; he still hadn't asked anything about Dad.

Fiona stood by the wall, twisting the phone cable

between her fingers. Jack and Beth exchanged glances; by the look on Fiona's face, whoever she was talking to wasn't happy. A faint whirring sound above him caused Jack to look up. Another camera. It rotated to point at him and Beth. He shivered. There was nothing dark and gloomy in this place, but it still gave him the creeps.

Fiona slipped the phone back on its hook. "I'm afraid I'm going to have to cut the tour short. Dr Blackstone wants to see me."

"Dr Blackstone? The director of all this?" Beth squeaked, glancing quickly at Jack. "Oh, I'd love to meet him."

Fiona frowned. "He is far too busy to see you." She started shepherding them along the corridor.

"The thing is," said Jack, as Beth elbowed him in the ribs and gesticulated wildly for him to say something. "Um . . . I need to see Dr Blackstone about my skin."

"Dr Blackstone doesn't have patients – he's a scientist. If you've got a medical problem you need to see your own doctor." Fiona's stride didn't falter as she glanced over at him, her eyes cool and impassive.

"That's the problem. The doctors can't help me. Dr Blackstone might be able to tell me where my dad is."

"Your dad?"

"Yes, Dr Tom Phillips. He used to work here. He's the

119

only one who can help me with my photosensitivity."

Fiona's pace quickened but Jack could have sworn something changed in her face when he mentioned Dad's name. "I thought you two wanted a tour for your school project, but now I find out you've got a different agenda. I don't know what prank you're pulling here, but I don't appreciate you wasting my time."

"It's not a prank!" said Beth, pulling at Jack's arm. "Look at this. You can see how bad his skin is. She shifted Jack's hair away from the top of his ear. "And his leg's worse."

A look familiar to Jack passed over Fiona's face – it was a look of disgust. He batted Beth's hand away, wishing she hadn't drawn attention to his skin.

"The best I can do is give Dr Blackstone your details. If he's able to help, he'll contact you, I'm sure."

Her heels clipped on the tiled floor as she sped along the white corridor, leaving the labs behind. Beth and Jack scuttled along beside her.

"Where does that go?" asked Beth, as they whizzed past a grey door with a large red No Entry sign nailed to it.

"It leads to the older buildings and Dr Blackstone's private lab."

"What does he have a private lab for?"

"For his own research," Fiona snapped. "Not that it's any of your business."

Jack gazed at her, startled. Fiona's face had blanched and her lips were pressed together so tightly they had practically disappeared, leaving a narrow strip of scarlet. Her eyes were ice cold slits, like a snake's.

They'd reached the end of the corridor and she picked up another phone next to a metal door and spoke sharply into it. "Can you escort our visitors off the premises?" They'd hardly been warmly welcomed when they'd first met her, but since speaking to Blackstone, Fiona's manner had become glacial. And Jack didn't like the way she said "escort off the premises" – it made them sound like criminals.

She replaced the phone and pushed open the door. A metal staircase led down to the ground.

"Neville will take you back to the gatehouse. You can hand your passes in there. Good luck with your project, if indeed such a thing exists." As the guard approached, she ducked back through the door and it slammed shut behind her.

"She's in a hurry to get away," murmured Beth as they walked over to the guard. "We'll ask Neville if he knew your dad. Security guards know everyone, don't they?"

"Good idea." Although he didn't like the thought of

talking to Neville. His grim face, bulging forearms and muscly frame were kind of off-putting. And he hadn't exactly wanted to talk to them earlier either.

"Never heard of him," the guard said as they stood in the gatehouse, waiting for the bus to arrive. He scrutinised Jack, a frown line appearing between his eyes.

"I need to find him. He used to work here fourteen years ago."

Neville stared at Jack. "I said I've never heard of him. You need to make an appointment with Dr Blackstone if you've got any questions with regards to former employees. I can't give out that information." The guard continued to glower at them. Jack and Beth had no choice but to shuffle away towards the bus, which had pulled up outside.

"He seriously looks as if he spends too long in the gym," muttered Beth. "You get on the bus. I'll ask these people if they knew your dad." She scooted off and as Jack clambered onto the bus Beth approached the line of people leaving the building. A few of them stopped, appeared to listen and then shrugged and moved on. Most of them darted out of her way or sloped past before she had a chance to speak to them. Eventually, Neville came out of the gatehouse and jerked his thumb at the bus. Beth climbed back on board, her mouth twisted down in a grimace.

"Nobody wanted to talk to me. In the end that bully Neville told me to get lost."

A ripple of disappointment washed over Jack. What had they found out from their visit? Precious little. Nobody wanted to talk about Dad and they hadn't managed to even get a glimpse of Blackstone.

"Blackstone will have to leave eventually," said Beth.

"Yeah, we'll stay and wait for him."

"Oh no you won't," said Beth, fixing him with a piercing gaze. "You said yourself there's not shade round here. You can't risk it. I'll hide out until he appears. Meet you at Lil's later."

Jack stared back at her and then gave a resigned shrug. What choice did he have? His stupid skin made it impossible for him to stay. Beth leapt off the bus, immediately making for some small bushes near the gatehouse.

The driver started his engine, ready to make the trip back to town. Jack turned to take one last look at Bioscience Discoveries. To his shock he found Neville gazing straight at him. The guard picked up the phone in the gatehouse. Jack couldn't drag his eyes away. His insides twisted into a knot. Still staring intently at him, Neville punched numbers into the phone and started to speak. There was no doubt in Jack's mind – the guard was talking about him.

Chapter Sixteen

Jack wasted the next couple of hours, while waiting for Beth to return, ringing phone numbers listed under Blackstone in Auntie Lil's phone book, and asking if a Richard lived there. That was until he remembered that research scientists probably didn't have their numbers or addresses in directories or online, in case nutters hassled them.

By the time Beth got back, he was feeling tetchy and tired.

"No luck," she said, as she slumped on the sofa next to him. "The man must be a workaholic. Either that or he left by a secret exit."

"I'm fed up with this. We'll go back to the lab tonight and hang around," said Jack with determination. "If we don't see him, we'll try and get inside."

"What's the point of doing that?" Beth gazed at him, open-mouthed. "What do you think we'll find? There's not going to be a ready-made cream on a shelf waiting for you. Even if there was, we don't know if a new cream is what you need."

"What do you mean by that?" he asked.

She shrugged but said nothing.

"Something's going on there," he said. "Did you see Fiona's face when I mentioned Dad's name and when you asked about the private lab? She's hiding something, I know it."

Beth stared at him, her forehead scrunched into a puzzled frown. "I didn't notice anything. She was just cross that we'd pretended to be researching a school project."

Jack shrugged. "All that 'do-good' research is a brilliant way of hiding what else is going on."

He couldn't explain how he felt to Beth. Some urge was propelling him onwards. Yes, he wanted to find Dad and get the help he needed for his out-of-control allergy. But he also needed to know what Dad had been involved in.

"I want a proper look round. I'm not going to get info any other way. It might be the key to finding Dad. If we meet Blackstone face-to-face he might listen to me. I can't wait weeks for an appointment."

"He's not likely to be hanging around in the middle of the night, is he? And how are we going to get inside? The security guards must be on duty twenty-four seven. Who knows what we'll find, and then there's your leg . . ." Beth's voice sounded so shaky, Jack glanced at her in surprise.

"My leg feels much better with the painkillers. And the antiseptic will start working soon. I'll manage; I have to. But you don't have to come with me if you don't want to." Jack was puzzled. He couldn't work Beth out. She was usually the optimist, the one to spur him into action, but that girl had vanished. "What's the matter?"

"It's been kind of exciting, up till now." Beth's eyes looked red and shiny. She fiddled with her hands in her lap, twisting her fingers together.

"I'm glad you've found it entertaining," said Jack, drily.

"But this is serious stuff," she continued. "It's madness to go in there. Things could go wrong. We'd be breaking the law – what if we get caught? We'd be turned over to the police. And it won't help find your dad."

Great. She'd got cold feet. He'd assumed she'd think the same as him, that she'd fall in with his plan.

"You were the one who said we should try and see Blackstone. Now you're saying the opposite. I thought you wanted to help."

"I do, but . . ." She fidgeted with the straps of her rucksack. "Look, creeping around at night is going too far."

"I can go on my own," he said, flatly. "I shouldn't drag you into this; it's my problem, not yours."

"I'm not scared for me, you idiot," she mumbled, her cheeks going pink. "It's you I'm worried about. I'm beginning to get used to you and I don't want it to be messed up. I've already lost two people I care about."

He gulped, heat seeping up his cheeks. It hadn't occurred to him that Beth might have a problem with his plan because of what had happened to her parents. That she might actually like him enough to be worried for him.

"And . . ." She hesitated. "Ever since we found that stuff out at the library, you've been a bit strange."

"Strange?" What was she talking about?

"Look, I want you to find your dad, but don't get too hung up on believing the lab has all the answers. I'm not sure getting inside is going to help. And . . ." she took a deep, trembling breath, "all the worry could be making your skin worse."

Jack snorted. He couldn't believe she was being so

unhelpful.

"Just saying," she said, not meeting Jack's eyes. "It's something to think about."

"I have to do this, Beth." He coughed to disguise the wobble in his own voice. "I know it's risky but I've got to try. Look at me. My skin's a mess. Time's running out and it's the only idea I've got. But I'll understand if you don't want to come."

So, that's that, Jack thought to himself, as the silence between them lengthened. He'd be on his own.

But then Beth took a deep breath and said, "Okay, I'll come with you. But on two conditions."

"What're they?"

"First: we find a way to get inside without breaking in. Second: if we don't find any answers, you tell your mum about your allergy getting worse. No excuses."

"Agreed. But you're sure you want to come?"

Beth gave a weak smile. "You'll need someone to hold your hand."

Heat whooshed up his face at the thought of her hand in his, the gloom that had begun to seep through his bones disappearing as fast as it had come. Despite saying he'd understand if she didn't come, he was secretly pleased. He liked having her around – and he didn't want to admit it, but he was scared. The idea of getting caught was frightening enough, but the thought of what he might discover in the labs petrified him.

Chapter Seventeen

Beth went to take a shower. Jack was glad to have a bit of space to think things through. Was he crazy to contemplate going to Bioscience Discoveries in the middle of the night? Probably, but what else could he do? Pretend he hadn't found out about the experiments? Forget about finding Dad? He sighed heavily as he heaved himself up from the sofa. He couldn't think straight when he was hungry and it was ages since he'd eaten breakfast.

"Auntie Lil!" he called out as he made his way into the hall. "Do you want a sandwich?"

No response. A deep humming noise drifted from upstairs. Jack hobbled up the steps and made his way along the landing. The humming grew louder as he approached the spare room Beth used.

"What a mess!" Auntie Lil switched off the hoover when she caught sight of Jack and showed him a pile of dust which lay on the floor. "I can't begin to imagine what Beth's been doing in here."

Jack stared in horror, mesmerised by the sight of the remains of Beth's parents sprinkled over the carpet and Auntie Lil with the hoover. He was sure this wasn't the kind of scattering Beth had in mind. An ash trail snaked its way from Auntie Lil's feet to Beth's bed. The trail ended next to the unzipped rucksack which Beth must have stuffed under the bed before she had her shower.

"I'll need a dustpan and brush," she said, putting down the hoover pipe. "I don't want to ruin the cleaner with this grit."

Jack thought fast; no way could he let Auntie Lil throw the ashes away. Beth would go mad if she found out. "Don't worry, I'll tidy it up."

Auntie Lil's eyebrows crinkled together as she looked at him. "If you're sure. It is a little late in the day for me to start cleaning."

"Maybe we shouldn't mention the mess to Beth," he added. "She might be embarrassed having made it."

"Hmmm," said Auntie Lil, folding her arms across her chest. "I think you need to tell me what's going on here."

Jack opened his mouth to protest that nothing was going on, but Auntie Lil fixed her stern gaze on him. "You don't fool me, Jack. I expect you to tell me when you've cleared up."

Jack sighed and then nodded. After Auntie Lil had left the room, he grabbed Beth's bag, yanked the zip down the rest of the way and peered inside. The lid of one of the wooden urns gaped open, the clasp slightly bent out of shape. He lifted both boxes out, put them to one side and dug around inside the bag. Then he tipped it upside down over the open box and a handful of ashes trickled out. Now all he had to worry about were those on the floor. He started scooping them up with his hands and pouring them into the box. He worked quickly, aware Beth could appear at any second.

Once he had gathered up as much as he could, he looked inside the urn; his heart sank. It contained barely half the ashes it used to have. A crazy idea entered his head: he could remove dust from the hoover bag and shovel that in too. But, somehow, it didn't seem right to mix Beth's mum with household dirt. So he pressed the faulty clasp back into shape, shut the box and placed it carefully in her rucksack. He lifted the bag to test its weight, swearing under his breath – Beth was bound to notice it was lighter than it used to be.

133

He carried the dustpan and brush into the kitchen where Auntie Lil was making a cup of tea. Beth hadn't reappeared yet.

"So," she said, pouring water into the pot. "What was that all about?"

Jack's heart began to pound. What should he say? Beth had trusted him with her secret but Auntie Lil was perfectly capable of packing him off home if she sensed he was lying to her. And then there would be no chance to investigate Bioscience Discoveries.

He took a deep breath. "Her parents' ashes."

Auntie Lil's mouth fell open. "Ashes? Why on earth is she carrying them around?"

Jack shrugged.

"This is dreadful. She needs to be told what happened. I should speak to her—"

"No!" The word came out more forcefully than he'd intended.

Auntie Lil paused, her crinkled eyes regarding him kindly. "Somebody needs to. Perhaps it'd be better coming from you?"

Jack nodded. His mind turned over a dozen thoughts simultaneously. Beth had spent the last two years carrying those boxes. She'd go ballistic if she found out that half the ashes were missing. He wasn't going to be the one to tell her. At least not right then. He'd wait – wait until after the trip to the labs. Find a way to break the news to her gently. He didn't want her to freak out – he'd come to rely on her confidence when he felt shaky.

Entering the sitting room he gazed around, spotting a glass paperweight he'd bought for Auntie Lil when he was on holiday with Mum and Dad in Cornwall a few years ago. He picked it up, rotating the weight in his hand. The glass was cool, heavy and smooth like velvet. Different shades of blue, green and scarlet swirled together in the centre of the dome, creating a kaleidoscope of colour. He hurried as fast as he could back upstairs and jammed it in the bottom of Beth's bag.

*

That night, Jack found himself skulking in the bushes with Beth, outside the perimeter fence of the laboratory. They had sneaked out of the house while Auntie Lil slept. Jack knew, once she went to bed, she rarely stirred before morning. Twice, though, he'd gone to wake Beth up only to hear Auntie Lil still moving around in her room. Eventually, they'd caught the late bus and got off at Selchester, realising it was safer to walk the rest of the way. By the time they got to the site, one a.m. had come and gone.

To Jack's dismay, Beth had brought her rucksack with

her.

"It goes where I go," she'd said as they got ready to leave Auntie Lil's house. There was no persuading her otherwise.

They spent the next hour peering through the thicket, watching for any sign of Blackstone. Eventually they had to admit they couldn't wait any longer. Blackstone was either not coming out or had gone home. And this was despite the fact Beth had spotted what they thought was his car in the car park – registration plate BL09ACK.

Time for plan B. On their last visit Jack had spied an open window high up in one of the older buildings. This was how he imagined getting inside and keeping his promise to Beth – technically, going through an open window wasn't breaking in. And if everything went to plan, no one would know they'd even been there.

He'd told Beth if it was shut they'd leave. Trouble was, however hard he squinted, he couldn't see if the window was still open.

"How are we going to get past the guard and security cameras?" whispered Beth.

"If we stay out of the light the cameras won't pick us up." Jack spoke confidently, but his insides felt as though they'd turned to mush. He had no idea if the cameras were infrared or not. If they were, they'd be in trouble.

"What if the fence is electrified?"

"It's not," he said. "There aren't any of those connector things. I checked when we were here earlier. The window's under that wall. Hopefully we'll find a way to climb up."

"And if we can't?"

Jack shrugged. He hadn't planned that far ahead. He wished Beth would shut up – it was as if she was trying to think of obstacles to stop them doing this. In the gloom her face appeared deathly white – partly from her make-up and partly from fear, he guessed. He realised his hand was trembling; he wiped a sweaty palm on his trousers.

The guard, a different one to earlier, sat in the gatehouse listening to the radio. Jack picked up the faint music drifting towards them on the soft night breeze. They had already watched him do two inspections of the perimeter fence, swinging his bright torch in a wide arc, from right to left. Each time he'd taken ten minutes to walk around the site and back to the gatehouse.

They waited. At last, after what seemed like an age, the security guard re-emerged from his hut. Jack held his breath as yet again he passed by their hiding place. The second he'd turned the corner they sprinted to the three-metre-high fence and clambered up. The climb was fairly easy as the wire links provided plenty of finger and toe holds. Jack had brought an old sweatshirt with him which he hurled across the barbed wire at the top. He scrambled over, dropped onto the ground on the other side and dashed towards one of the older buildings. Beth followed him. At various intervals, lights illuminated the pathways around the site. They hugged the walls to avoid being suddenly exposed.

Jack came to a stop and peered upwards. This was the right spot. He inspected the wall, running his hand over it. Ivy covered the rough bricks but wasn't strong enough to use like rope. Then his hand hit something hard and cold. Good. A thick drainpipe. Jack gave it a tug; it felt strong. He positioned his hands above the first bracket and heaved himself up.

The climb was harder than he'd expected. He had to rely on touch to find handholds. The pipe kept slipping through his fingers. His leg throbbed and he desperately wanted to scratch the scab on his hand which had started to itch again.

I must be mad, he thought, cursing himself for coming up with such a stupid plan. Too late to change his mind now.

Every fifteen seconds the beam of a security light swung across the buildings, hitting the wall less than a metre above him. He waited, clinging to the pipe like a monkey to a tree, pressing his body against it to make himself as invisible as possible, until the beam had passed. Then he clambered on, praying he'd make it past before the beam made its return trip. He had no way to warn Beth about the searchlight. He hoped she'd seen it. He struggled on until he reached the top and lay flat against the roof tiles. A clang pierced the silence, then a dog barked. He froze, heart in mouth – he'd forgotten about the Alsatian. A few seconds later Beth's head popped up next to him. A surge of relief rushed over him.

As soon as he saw she was safe, Jack started slithering on his belly along the sloping roof. They couldn't risk standing, they'd be seen; but the darkness made their progress slow. Jack tried to ignore the pain in his leg; each move he made caused a stabbing pain like the twist of a knife. He hoped he wasn't making the wound worse. How would he cope if blood gushed all over the place? He felt sick at the thought.

Finally, they reached the part of the roof directly above the window. He tipped his head over the guttering to have a look. A faint light glowed from inside but the frosted glass meant he had no idea what lay on the other side. To his relief, the top pane was ajar, but Jack gazed at it in alarm. The gap was tiny. It would be a tight squeeze. Beth removed her rucksack.

"Hold onto my legs," she instructed.

She lay as flat as she could and lowered her arms onto the frame. She rattled the pane, trying to prise it open further, grunting from the effort. Jack gripped her tightly. He glanced over in the direction of the gatehouse. The dog barked again. Nearer this time.

"Hurry," he whispered.

A couple of minutes passed. The dog was barking frantically now. Had they been spotted?

"That's wide enough." She turned round, stomach on the tiles, and lowered her legs into the opening while Jack held onto her arms.

"I'm in." Most of her body was through the gap, so Jack let go.

Her head and arms disappeared.

Chapter Eighteen

There was a loud thud.

Jack waited. And waited. A minute passed.

He began to panic, wondering what he should do if Beth didn't reappear.

"Beth . . . Beth?" he hissed.

"I'm okay," a muffled voice came from inside the room. She appeared at the window. "Your turn."

Jack passed her rucksack through and dropped his legs into the opening, grasping the guttering in his fingers. His feet waggled, trying to find something solid. A touch from Beth's hands steadied him as he planted his feet on a hard surface and slid the rest of his body through the gap.

There was no mistaking where he was. He was standing on the lid of a toilet in a small cubicle, with barely enough space for them both.

"You're lucky. I put it down for you." Beth showed him a wet shoe and leggings. Jack gave her a nervous grin and jumped down, wincing as he did so. He balanced with one foot on the lid and rolled up his trouser leg to inspect his shin. The bandage looked yellow which was bad news. It meant the injury had opened again, but at least there wasn't any sign of bleeding. Yet.

"Sshh!" Beth put her fingers to her lips.

Jack froze, heart pounding against his ribcage. He heard the heavy tread of footsteps. Somebody stopped outside. Beth seized hold of his clammy hand. A glimmer of torchlight appeared in the gap at the bottom of the door.

"All's fine here. Over."

The sound of radio static filled the air and then a crackling voice uttered a garbled, fuzzy reply.

The footsteps strode away again. Jack realised he'd been holding his breath. He exhaled slowly through his mouth.

"That was close," whispered Beth. "Do you think they saw us on the cameras?"

He shrugged, seriously spooked. "We need to get out of here before we're found."

Beth pushed the door open, craned her neck to look

both ways and stepped out of the tiny room. Jack followed. He found himself standing in the middle of a long, empty corridor that faded into the darkness in both directions. The dim emergency lights high up on the panelled ceiling did nothing to dispel the gloom. He switched on the torch he'd brought with him. A line of grey doors stretched left and right, all of them closed. The area felt different to where they'd been that afternoon. It was cramped and narrow, the ceiling lower. The walls seemed to close in on him. It was like being in an illusion museum, where the rooms felt as if they were tilting at a weird angle.

No sign of any security cameras as far as he could see. The bitter smell of disinfectant and chemicals hit his nose and the back of his throat, making him want to cough. He swallowed hard to stifle it.

"What are we looking for?" Beth gazed around.

"I'm not sure. Maybe Blackstone's office or private lab – anything which might tell us what's going on here."

They walked along the corridor, their footsteps echoing on the concrete floor. As they passed each door, they rattled the handles. Locked.

"This is impossible," said Beth. "We don't even know if we're in the right building. Let's leave, Jack. I don't like it."

"Not yet," said Jack. "Let's go down to the floor below." He didn't want to give up, having spent all that effort getting inside.

Finding themselves in an identical corridor, they tried each door, but again they were locked or opened into storage cupboards. Finally they reached the last one. Jack could see a splash of bluish light spilling out through the crack at the bottom. He jiggled the handle, not expecting it to budge, but this time, to his surprise, it turned.

"Wait!" Beth put her hand on top of his to stop him. "What's that?"

Jack paused a moment. His breathing became shallow and fast as he listened. High-pitched screeching noises filtered through the closed door. He and Beth stared at each other in horror. It sounded as if something or someone was in unimaginable pain.

Chapter Nineteen

The shrieking came from cages stacked on top of a metal counter that ran along the far wall of the laboratory. From where he stood, Jack could see dark shapes scurrying backwards and forwards, red eyes glinting in the torchlight. They edged closer, Beth keeping her fingers firmly in her ears.

Jack peered into one of the cages. It housed two white rats, or rather they must have once been white, looking at what remained of their fur. But each had pink patches of skin showing through and several of these bare areas had developed red sores. He almost retched from the smell – like rotting meat.

The animals, so noisy when they first entered the room, had calmed down and apart from the occasional squeak were quiet.

"Lab rats. They've been experimented on," said Jack, an icy coldness enveloping his body. "Do you notice anything strange about their sores?"

"Like what?" Beth came over to join him, her shocked expression mirroring his own.

"They're like the ones on the dog."

"But who would experiment on a pet? Rats and mice – yeah. I've read loads in my magazines about testing drugs on animals. But pets?" Beth shook her head. "I don't get it."

And children. Who would experiment on children? the faint voice muttered inside Jack.

"Is this Blackstone's private lab?" said Beth, looking around. "The one Fiona told us about?"

"Guess so."

"Look at this!" called Beth. She'd moved to a long workbench in the middle of the lab. The bench housed a mess of test tubes, jars of chemicals and other pieces of equipment. Piles of books lay in a stack on the floor and on one of the lab stools and a tower of cardboard file boxes teetered on the edge of the bench. A potion gurgled away in a container over a flame. Jack swallowed nervously, wiping a sleeve across his eyes. Soon somebody would be coming back to finish their experiment. Beside all this stuff sat a mound of paperwork. Beth held a sheet of paper in her hand.

"It's a report," she said, moving nearer the lamp. "About the rats." She went quiet, causing Jack to glance at her.

His heart skipped a beat as he snatched the paper from her.

The report contained a heap of scientific data, most of which he didn't understand, and it wasn't until he reached the final paragraph that he found some information he could make any sense of. He pointed it out to Beth who read it aloud, running her finger underneath the words. "The rats treated with the anti-ageing serum, without exception, have shown an adverse reaction to sunlight, resulting in sores, rashes and hair loss. This new set of trials shows that no further progress has been made to eradicate these serious side effects."

"They're sensitive to sunlight, like me!" Jack bit his lip. "I've got exactly the same symptoms, apart from the thing with the hair." Of course! That's what he'd found so troubling about the dog on the side of the road. Its skin reminded him of his own. Jack gazed at Beth in disbelief. He realised he was trembling. "What if those rumours in the newspaper were true? What if Dad experimented on children with this, what's it called, 'anti-ageing serum'?

What if I was one of them?"

His legs started to buckle underneath him and a spasm of pain shot down his injured leg. He needed to sit before he collapsed onto the floor. Beth seized his arm and propelled him towards a stool. "It might be a coincidence. And there are loads of causes of photosensitivity. Just because you've got an allergy to sunlight as well, doesn't mean you were experimented on. There's no mention of children in the report, is there?"

None of this made Jack feel any better. A lump had developed in his throat. He thought he was going to burst into tears.

"It's all falling into place," he said. "The rumours, the newspaper reports, Dad having to leave, the rats and my skin. Everything. And it looks as though they're still doing the research – which means Blackstone must be in on it."

"Do you really believe that your dad would hurt you?" Beth shook her head in exasperation or something else, he didn't care what. His brain was too full to listen to what she was saying.

Jack rubbed his hand over his eyes, angrily brushing at the tears that had welled up and threatened to fall.

"No . . . I don't know."

"We'd better go," said Beth in a quiet voice. "I hate

this place."

Suddenly she froze. The rats had started their squealing again.

"Quick!" she said. "I think someone's coming."

They managed to duck behind the bench as somebody entered the lab. There was a click and a light came on.

A stool scraped across the floor. "I could do with a coffee," a man's voice said. "Want one?"

There was a grunt, and the door opened and closed again. The rustling of papers was followed by a loud yawn.

Jack looked at Beth as they crouched behind the bench, hardly daring to breathe. The door creaked opened again, followed by the sound of clinking mugs.

"It's time I dealt with these rats since there's no sign of improvement. We don't want to risk contamination of the healthy ones," the same man said, his voice coming from over by the cages. There was another scrape of the stool and the sound of footsteps moving in the same direction.

Jack grabbed Beth's hand and, still half squatting, pulled her towards the door. He tugged it open, twisting round to glance behind him as he did so. The two men stood looking in the cages. It was the taller one who caught his attention even though he had his back to Jack: lanky, long legs and a mop of unruly dark hair. Suddenly all the blood seemed to rush from Jack's body.

"Dad?"

Both men spun round, their eyes opening wide as they clocked Jack and Beth.

Chapter Twenty

In that split second Jack realised his mistake. It looked like Dad from the back, but it wasn't him. The men's eyes registered first shock and then anger, as Jack attempted to get his wobbly legs to work. He stumbled against the doorframe and almost collapsed in a heap before Beth jerked him out of the room. They shot along the corridor, making their way towards the stairs, but loud voices from further on halted their progress.

"In here." Beth nipped through a doorway to a cupboard they'd passed earlier. Mops, buckets, rolls of toilet paper and bottles of cleaning fluid crowded in on Jack as he pushed inside. Beth pulled the door closed, plunging them into a stifling blackness. The only sounds were her quick, shallow breaths and the blood pounding in his ears.

Footsteps approached and stopped outside.

Jack pressed his ear against the door to listen. A muffled voice came from the other side.

"You go downstairs and I'll search along here. They can't have got far. I've alerted the gate, so they won't be able to escape that way."

Jack heard the footsteps moving away. What should they do? If they left the relative safety of the cupboard they'd definitely be spotted. Maybe it would be better to wait a while, until the guards had thought they'd escaped.

But after ten minutes of standing in a cramped, stuffy cupboard that stank of cleaning fluid, trying not to make a noise, they'd both had enough.

"We'll have to take the risk," he whispered.

He pushed the door and peeped through the crack. There was no sign of the men. He stepped out and beckoned for Beth to follow.

"Hey!" A sudden shout made them spin around. A security guard stood at the far end of the corridor, blocking their escape route. Panic froze Jack to the spot. The guard had a growling dog on a lead at his side.

Jack fled in the opposite direction, Beth beside him. The man's footsteps followed. And the clicking of sharp claws on the floor. Heavy panting pursued them as they pelted along.

"Faster!" yelled Jack. He threw a look behind him. The dog's frothing mouth and sharp teeth were gaining on them with every step.

Then the passageway split into two.

"Which way?" Beth gasped.

Jack hesitated, fear numbing his brain. Out of the corner of his eye, he caught sight of an illuminated fire exit sign off to the right.

"This way!" he shouted, pointing to the sign, and they set off again, at full speed. Jack tugged the door to the fire exit open; a narrow stairway faced him with steps leading up and down.

"Somebody's coming." Beth's eyes widened with alarm, the unmistakable thud of pounding feet rising up the stairwell.

"We go up," said Jack, praying the door wouldn't be locked at the top. He scrambled upwards, taking two steps at a time, not caring how much noise he made and ignoring the searing pain in his leg. He panted, painful gasping breaths struggling through his narrow windpipe.

They reached the last step. Jack shoved the heavy fire door, pushing on the metal bar that ran along its length. It groaned and creaked, but thankfully swung outwards. They tumbled into the warm air.

They were at the top of the building, on a flat, asphalted part of the roof. Jack was shocked to see a red glow peeping between the trees. Sunrise loomed. More time must have passed than he'd imagined. But for him the sunlight was another complication and he wasn't wearing his cream.

His eyes scanned the roof for something with which to barricade the door, until they fell upon an old broom a workman must have left up there. He rushed to the door as the dog slammed against it, pushing it open a crack. Its teeth were pulled back in a snarl, saliva spraying from its cavernous mouth. He wrestled the door shut again. The guard called out but Jack took no notice. He jammed the broom handle through the bar and under the lock. It wouldn't hold for long, but maybe long enough for them to figure out a way off the roof.

He hurried to the railings and looked over, hoping for a drainpipe or an escape ladder. No such luck. An iron platform abutted the area and led out onto a steeply sloping glass roof. At the end, ten metres away, Jack noticed a small window, open about twenty centimetres. Beyond that he could see the leafy tops of trees and a bank of orangey-pink cloud as the sun crept over the horizon.

"We'll have to go over the glass to reach that window."

"Jack!" Something in Beth's voice made him reel round. She was holding her side and grimacing. Jack could see her shoulders heaving up and down as she struggled to get the words out. "Why don't we give ourselves up?"

He shook his head. "We can do this. It's not far." A banging and pounding from the direction of the door made Jack grab hold of Beth's hand and hurry her onto the iron platform.

"Is it safe?" He followed her wide-eyed gaze and took in the sheer panes of glass that stretched between where they stood and the open window. It was like a huge glass conservatory. Thin steel frames separated the giant panes. From the platform a ladder led downwards hugging the panes until it reached the edge of the roof, where a line of glass bricks rose up to form a parapet. No chance for shadow jumping here – shade was non-existent. "Can it take our weight?"

"If we step on the frames next to the parapet we'll be fine," said Jack with a confidence he didn't feel.

He glanced towards the window; a beam of sunlight was creeping up the roof towards it. So little time.

"Ready?" He looked at her.

She shuddered and then gave a tight-lipped smile. "You first."

He stepped onto the thin strip of frame, expecting it to creak under his weight, but nothing happened. He placed his other foot on the glass parapet. With one foot on there and the other on the narrow frame he shuffled along.

Loud thumps and bangs from behind made him realise he was moving too slowly. He looked at the parapet running alongside and gingerly stepped onto it. He caught sight of the ground falling away below him. Dizziness overwhelmed him for a second. He had a sudden flashback to slipping from the roof and Beth stretching out her arm to save him. That seemed like a lifetime ago.

To his other side, he looked down on a series of open-plan offices. In one, two cleaners worked, wiping desks and emptying bins. He stopped to take a few deep breaths and, looking forwards, concentrated on placing one foot in front of the other as if walking on a tightrope. He stretched his arms out to the sides to steady himself and moved across the glass, not daring to look behind to check on Beth. As he progressed he felt his muscles loosen, the tension dropping from his body. He could do this, he thought, as his movements became more fluid and steady.

Although it was early morning, the air had turned muggy already. Beads of sweat started to form on his forehead, trickling down his face. His shirt felt as if it was soldered to his chest. The sun's rays caused pinpricks of pain on his back and top of his skull. He tried not to think about whether his skin was frying.

Jack stopped and scuffled round to face the glass roof, his heels overhanging the parapet. Here the opaque glass made it impossible to see what was beneath him. He stretched out his arms, leaning forwards, but he couldn't reach the window. He looked behind him. The ground was a long way down. No escape that way. He shifted his gaze back to the window – he needed to concentrate. Now was not the time to freak out.

He shook his hands by his sides, puffed out his cheeks and blew through his mouth. Then he launched himself towards the window, arms stretched in front, fingers splayed. He caught hold of the frame, his body slamming into the glass.

"Ugh!" The breath rushed out of his lungs. The metal dug into the flesh on his fingers. For a moment he hung from the frame, his feet grappling with the slippery glass, trying to get enough grip to heave himself up. His top had ridden up and the early morning sun struck his back. Fierce rays bounced off the roof, hitting his skin and creating pockets of burning pain.

How long had he been out there? Seconds? Minutes? He heard a faint popping noise – was that his skin blistering or the roof expanding from the heat? He had to move. Fast. Ignoring the agony from the stretched muscles in his arms, he pulled himself towards the opening, his legs kicking and shoes slipping on the panes. He manoeuvred his head through the window and then his arms and shoulders.

Easing the rest of his body through the small gap, he dropped onto a table in the empty office below. He sank onto his haunches, arms wrapped around his knees, waiting for his breathing to return to normal and for his legs to stop shaking.

A minute later a thud came from outside the window. The grey, cloudy outline of Beth's body appeared, flattened against the glass. Straightening up, he stuck his head through the window. She pushed her rucksack towards him. As he jerked it inside, a creaking and whirring noise started above his right ear.

"Window's shutting," he shouted. He reached as far as he could and grasped her hands tightly. His torso was half out the window as he balanced on his toes to tug her. Her legs and feet thrashed against the glass as she tried to propel herself up and through the gap. Jack felt the frame brush against his back as it attempted to close. With one massive heave, he managed to haul her up the final part. He pulled himself back inside to allow her body to slip through the remaining narrow gap and thump onto the table next to him.

"This way." He jumped from the table, squeezed between two large, polished wooden desks and vaulted over a swivel chair. He tore towards the door, only for it to crash open in front of him.

"Watch out, Jack!"

His body stiffened as a large figure clothed in black loomed over him. The man seized him before he could dart out of the way, clamping his arms by his sides. Another guard swiftly entered the room and grabbed Beth. Jack twisted this way and that, the air being pressed out of his body by the iron grip. His lungs felt as if they were about to explode as he struggled to breathe. With one final wrench, he managed to twist free of the man's grasp. But his body was off balance and as he reeled away, he stumbled.

The last thing he remembered was the desk rushing up to meet him. Then darkness fell.

Chapter Twenty-One

"Geroff! Leave me alone!"

"Wake up, Jack!" A voice called him, the sound faint and muffled.

Jack groaned. He thought he was going to be sick. He opened his eyes a slit. Blurry shapes whirled in front of him. He shook his head, trying to clear his vision, then blinked rapidly, his lids scratching over dry eyeballs. His mouth felt as if he'd been chewing on cardboard and his skull throbbed like it'd been split in two with a cleaver.

He was lying in a small room on a metal trolley bed, like the kind found in a hospital. With relief he realised he could move his legs and arms.

A single light bulb, hanging above him from the centre of the ceiling, cast a weak yellowish glow. A kind of metal workbench ran round the sides of the small room with glass-fronted cabinets hanging above it. A faint smell of disinfectant hung in the air along with another disgusting stench. Looking down, Jack realised it came from him – a kidney-shaped cardboard sick dish lay next to him on the bed, a foul yellow liquid swimming in the bottom. He moaned – looking in the bowl made him want to throw up again.

"Are you okay?" asked Beth. She sat on a chair beside him, her white face streaked with dirt and tears. Her black make-up had smudged to create two dark panda circles around her eyes.

"What happened?" He heaved himself up into a sitting position.

"You knocked yourself out on the desk. The guards carried you here." Her voice was etched with weariness and worry. She flopped back in her seat, rubbing her tired eyes. "They'll be coming back in a minute with a doctor."

"I feel weird." Numb, that's what he actually felt.

"You're bound to – after being knocked out."

Panic surged through his body. They'd been caught – who knew what they would do to them now. He struggled to twist round and place his feet on the ground. "How are we going to get out of here?"

Beth was strangely silent. Jack guessed she was trying

to think of some comforting words to help him. But what was there to say? His dad, the great scientist, had experimented on him, he was convinced. He was willing to risk his son's life for the sake of an anti-ageing drug. Jack had no idea whether it was for money or fame or to save his reputation as a scientist. It didn't matter why; the fact was he didn't care about his family. A sharp twinge shot up his damaged shin – Dad didn't care about him.

And would being given an anti-ageing drug mean he'd live longer than anyone else? Or would he endure more horrible side effects? One thing was certain, there was no point living longer if he spent it in Blackstone's clutches. And he owed it to Beth to get her out of the mess he'd created. Blackstone couldn't keep them locked up. For one thing, they would start to be missed. Jack's heart skipped a beat: Auntie Lil. She would be fretting; perhaps she'd already called the police. He reached in his pocket for his phone. Then, with a heart as heavy as marble, he remembered the shattered fragments lying on his bedroom floor.

He struggled to his feet, his legs almost crumpling underneath him as nausea swept over him. He scuffled to the door and jiggled the handle.

"I've already checked that," said Beth, from her position slumped in the chair. "It's locked. They said it was a precaution; they want the doctor to see you. They're only going to be gone a few minutes." She looked exhausted, as if all the fight had left her.

"Sorry," said Jack, as he slid to the floor by the door.

"What for?"

"Sorry for getting you into this mess. I shouldn't have made you come."

"Hey, you didn't make me come. I wanted to. None of this is your fault." Beth came over and sat next to him. He buried his head in his hands and an uncontrolled sob racked his body. Then he realised with a start Beth was talking to him.

"They've taken it – if they've touched them I'll . . ."

"What are you talking about?"

"My rucksack. They've got it."

A red cloud settled over Jack and a huge wave of anger threatened to erupt from inside. "Is that all you can worry about? Here we are stuck in some hole, nobody has a clue where we are and all you care about is your stupid rucksack."

"There's no need to be like that." Beth turned her frightened face towards his.

"Yeah, there is. Why are you so bothered about those ashes? It's not like they're all there anyway." An ominous silence followed these words and as soon as they left his mouth he wanted to bite them back. He wished he could crawl into a deep, dark hole and never come out. "Sorry," he mumbled, the hot burst of anger cooling as soon as it had gushed out. "I shouldn't have said that."

"What did you mean?"

"Forget it. I didn't mean anything."

Beth glared at him, her pale, grimy face drained of colour. He squirmed under her gaze. "Tell me."

He swallowed nervously. "The ashes came out of one of the urns yesterday and Auntie Lil accidently hoovered them up."

"That's one sick joke, Jack."

"It's true."

"And when were you going to tell me?" She looked at him. "Oh, I see. Waiting till I'd helped you with your stupid plan, huh? Well, thanks a bunch."

"I didn't want to upset you."

"Yeah, right. How do you think I feel now?"

He flushed – why had he let anger get the better of him? He wanted to comfort her, put an arm round her, but he didn't think she'd want him anywhere near. Her reaction to his outburst alarmed him. Before this idiotic scheme to investigate the lab, she'd have thumped him for saying something like that – it was still fresh in his mind how she'd reacted to Kai on the roof. Now she looked like a deflated balloon. Her face was pinched and closed; even worse a tear had appeared and rolled down her cheek.

"Listen, I'm sorry – I shouldn't have said anything. Not all of the ashes are gone. I managed to sweep most of them up." An oppressive silence followed, one which Jack wanted desperately to break, but he didn't know how. It was his own fault – he'd messed up.

"I've always blamed myself," she eventually mumbled, wiping her face on her sleeve.

"Blamed yourself for what?"

"My parents' deaths."

Jack puckered his brow and then grimaced as a dull ache pulsed through his bruised forehead. "It was an accident."

Beth shook her head. "They were going to a party and left me at home with Ama, our neighbour. I was fed up with being left behind, so I got Ama to ring them saying I wasn't feeling well, even though I was fine. They turned round to come home and the lorry hit them on their way back. I kept thinking if I hadn't persuaded Ama I was ill, my mum and dad would still be alive today." She hugged her knees with her arms. "I've never talked to anyone about it before, not even Cathy."

Despite his guilt and worry a warm tingle spread

through his body. If he was the first person she'd told, maybe she thought him more than just a friend. "It wasn't your fault. It was fate or bad luck or something. Your parents wouldn't want you blaming yourself. You have to let it go."

"That's the trouble; I don't think I can." She sniffed and then pulled her shoulders back. "Sorry about the tears. I don't usually cry so easily."

Eager to do something – anything – Jack wandered around the room, which didn't take long. He fought to keep the anxiety and fear at bay, wrestling with his cotton wool brain to come up with a plan to get them out of the mess.

It soon became clear there was no way out apart from through the locked door. The cabinets were all padlocked and held nothing anyway which could help them escape. He sprawled on the bed and peeked at the bandage covering his leg. The brief glimpse of the yellow sticky covering made his stomach flip over.

"We need to get out of here," he said. "Before they come back."

"I think we should wait – those guards said you need to see a doctor. I don't think they'll do anything to hurt us."

"Are you crazy?" Jack looked at her in disbelief. "Are you seriously suggesting we wait to find out what they might do to us? They use children in experiments. Do you want that to happen to you?" Jack's voice had risen to a screech. He couldn't believe Beth wanted to sit and wait for some madman to use them as test subjects.

"I don't like to say this but you're being a tad OTT. We don't *know* anything, Jack. We shouldn't jump to conclusions without knowing the facts. What proof do we have? All we've got is the word of a dodgy man who sweeps the streets and some articles in a shoddy newspaper."

"We've got me. *I'm* the proof! What's with you anyway? You've changed your tune. All that stuff about investigating this place – meeting Blackstone."

"That was before."

"Before what?"

"Oh I don't know, Jack – before you went all weird and wanted to snoop around in here. Look, if we apologise, they might let us go with a warning. They didn't seem that scary to me."

"You've got to be kidding." Jack glared at her. "They're not going to let us go. We know their secret."

Beth lowered her smudged eyes and pressed her lips together as if to prevent words tumbling from her mouth.

"A dead dog, rats with the same symptoms as me, secret labs . . . what more evidence do you need?"

"Okay, okay, stop being so stressy." Beth chewed her lip. "I know it *looks* bad. What do you have in mind, Houdini?"

Jack ignored Beth's comment. "I wait beside the door and jump on him. You could . . ."

"I could kick him where it hurts," said Beth. "Then we run."

"It's not brilliant." Jack sighed. "But it might work."

They didn't have long to wait to put the plan into action, as at that moment keys rattled in the lock.

"Quick! Get ready!" whispered Jack as he stood up and clenched his fists. He moved towards the door and waited. Beth took up position next to him.

The heavy, solid door thudded open and a shadowy figure emerged from the gloom outside.

Chapter Twenty-Two

"Steady on!" said a voice, as Jack launched his attack with flailing arms. "Stop. I need to talk to you."

As soon as he started Jack realised he didn't have the strength to continue. His legs wobbled and spots danced around at the edges of his vision. He glanced at Beth who hadn't moved from where she stood. Why didn't she help him? Backing away from the figure standing in the doorway, balled fists at his sides, he found the edge of the trolley bed and sat with a thump.

A man stood gazing at him, pale lips parted in a smile, his pointy, yellow teeth clearly visible. Jack recognised him instantly from the photo in the newspaper. Richard Blackstone's face was ingrained in his memory. He was obviously older, with lines etched across his temples and saggy, mottled skin under his chin. And instead of a suit he wore grey jogging pants and a white lab coat.

"Sorry we had to be so heavy-handed with you." Blackstone gestured to the door. "But I couldn't risk you running off again. Especially since you're injured."

He came and stood next to the bed and moved his toad-like face inches away from Jack's. He could see the hairs sprouting from the man's nostrils.

"First things first. Let's take a look at you." Blackstone made to move the hair where Jack had hurt himself. Jack flinched.

"I'm not going to hurt you. You've had a nasty fall and I need to examine you."

"To check I'm well enough for your experiments?" Jack said, his voice rasping with pain and fear.

Blackstone looked at him. "You need to be checked over. The ambulance will be here soon."

Jack snorted. What kind of game was Blackstone playing? As if he'd get an ambulance and allow him to leave. "Don't touch me."

"Perhaps you'd answer some questions then."

Jack glared at him.

"How many fingers am I holding up?"

Jack pointedly turned away.

"How old are you?"

Jack was silent. Blackstone would have to prise the information out of him.

"I'm trying to help you. I don't like being disturbed to attend to a teenager who's been caught trespassing. It's time to stop playing games. Now, what's your name?" Blackstone pulled up the seat next to him. "Well, perhaps if I start things off, it will prompt your memory. You're Tom's son. My PR Manager's briefed me on your visit today. She also told me you're looking for your dad. The question is, why would you think he's here?"

Beth piped up at this point. "We know he used to work here. His dad is the only one who can help him with his skin allergy. We thought we might find a clue as to where he is."

Blackstone regarded her with his tiny black eyes.

"I haven't seen Tom Phillips since he left fourteen years ago."

"We know all about your experiments on children," said Jack, unable to keep quiet any longer. "And on your dog."

"What are you talking about?"

"Don't deny it. It's in the newspapers. We've spoken to Ted Harris and seen the rats in your lab."

"Let me assure you, we have never carried out experiments on children," said Blackstone. "Those articles you read were based on rumours put out there by a disgruntled cleaner we sacked."

Jack sank back on the bed, resting on the thin pillow. His mind was buzzing, a mass of confused thoughts crashing together. Blackstone was lying – he had to be.

"Paramedics are here," a gruff voice said from the doorway.

Chapter Twenty-Three

Jack was vaguely aware of voices, whispers and slamming doors. He opened his eyes and found himself staring up at a white panelled ceiling. He must have dozed off. Confused, for one terrifying moment he thought he was back at the lab. Then he remembered he'd been taken in an ambulance. The metal bed he lay on was in hospital. One of those pulse monitor pegs was clipped to his finger with a beeping machine set up next to him, and the bed was surrounded by a flowery curtain. He'd been in the hospital all day under observation. Standard procedure for a bang on the head, the doctors said.

Everything that had happened over the last twenty-four hours came flooding back to him and he groaned. Dr Blackstone had ended up following the ambulance in his car and after the doctors had finished their examination he'd sat with Jack and Beth, answering their questions until Auntie Lil arrived. Jack cringed as memories of that conversation crowded in on him.

"Ted Harris was fired for incompetence – not disposing of equipment and used supplies in a safe manner," said Dr Blackstone. "I'm afraid his resentment boiled over and he went to the papers with a load of made-up stories, saying he'd witnessed things he hadn't seen. As he cleaned in the labs he'd noticed the rats your dad used in his experiments. He saw their blisters and, of course, he knew as everyone did about Tom and Maeve's child with the strange skin condition. Put the two together and what do you get? Over time Ted even began to believe his own lies."

Jack stared fixedly at the numbers on the monitor beside the bed – the figures slowly climbed as his pulse started to race. Blackstone made it all sound so plausible.

"Not much is needed to start rumours flying in a small community like this. As the chief scientist on the anti-ageing project, the press targeted your dad. The media is always trying to discredit the work we do here, and people are ready to believe what they say where experimentation is concerned. Your dad left because he couldn't stand the allegations circulating about him, even though none of it was true. It wasn't a pleasant time for him. He hated all the attention and negative comments he attracted when he walked along the street. And he didn't want the rumours to damage the company. Not that I cared about that. I knew the press would quickly lose interest, especially after the short-lived police investigation, but poor Tom couldn't take the pressure. He's a brilliant scientist but an extremely sensitive man. We were all devastated when he left."

"You didn't defend him, though, did you? The papers don't say anything about you standing up for him."

"Pah! The papers will write what they want, and leave out anything that doesn't suit their story. They'll do whatever it takes to sell their newspapers. If the front page read 'Blackstone Backs Renowned Scientist', would people have taken any notice of it? I doubt it. I tried to persuade your father to change his mind about leaving, but with no success, I'm afraid."

"My aunt says he had trouble getting another research job afterwards because of the rumours."

"Unlikely. Research companies are well-used to this type of situation and with his reputation he shouldn't have had any problems. However, the experience could have hurt him in other ways. Sometimes it's not outside factors that affect whether a person gets a job. It's what's happening inside them – their state of mind."

"What do you mean?"

"Like I said, your dad's sensitive. He took things to heart and couldn't let them go. He lost confidence. It's easy to do in this industry. I remember your dad as a perfectionist, a passionate scientist. Sometimes passion can get in the way of rational thought."

"Are you saying my dad went mad?"

"No, I'm saying he was probably suffering from stress."

Beth, who had been quiet all this time, gave a tiny gasp and shifted in her seat. "Can stress cause physical symptoms too?" she asked.

Blackstone smiled. "Ah, a budding scientist, I see. It's believed that stress can affect the body in many different ways."

Puzzled, Jack glanced at her, wondering what she was getting at, but he had his own question to ask. "What about my skin? You said Ted made the stories up, but I've got the same symptoms as the rats and Rex."

"Similar symptoms, not the same – that's the key. In medicine the little differences are important. For a start, you don't look as if you've had a problem with hair loss. The fact you suffer from a skin complaint is nothing to do with being given drugs from here. The rats you saw in my laboratory had side effects to the anti-ageing drugs I gave them – that much is true. We isolated them from the healthy rats, which we keep in a separate guarded area. Unfortunately, the sick rats haven't responded to treatment so we've decided to put them to sleep. When your dad left the company he left behind all his research. I've tried to continue what he started, but I'm nowhere near as brilliant as him. And we lost some of the funding for the project, so I've been using my own money, my own laboratory and my own time." He paused a second while he took his glasses off and wiped the lenses with a handkerchief from his pocket. "And what do you know about my dog?"

"The bus we were on ran it over," Beth said quietly. "When we got out to take a look we found sores all over its body."

Blackstone took a sharp intake of breath and dabbed his brow with the handkerchief before folding it neatly and putting it back in his pocket. "Rex escaped four weeks ago. I use a flat at the laboratories, in case I need to work at night, as I sometimes do – I thought he'd been stolen. He was probably suffering from mange, from running wild. That condition causes sores and scabs and can lead to hair loss."

"And your spies?" Jack whispered. "Ted told us about

them."

"Spies? Why would I have spies? Another of Ted's fantasies, I think."

"But Mrs Roberts . . ." Jack faltered. He was beginning to realise he'd made a colossal mistake. Everything he and Beth had investigated and found out over the last couple of days was based on a fragile web of lies and rumours. Rumours he'd been ready to believe. How could he have been so stupid? How could he have got so carried away? There had been no experimentation on children, nobody had been "watching" him. He hadn't seen Mrs Roberts in town, he just imagined he had. Ted wasn't the only one with an overactive imagination. "I . . . thought I was being spied on by my neighbour."

"What?" Beth gaped at him. "You didn't tell me that."

"Mrs Roberts has always been odd with me. And then when we were in town, she was there, lurking . . . I was sure it was her."

"*If* she was there, it had nothing to do with me." Blackstone stood up, stretching his spine as he did so. "I need to get back. I've got a long day in front of me and I'm not as young as I once was." He placed a hand on Jack's shoulder. "Things will be clearer when you're rested. Sometimes the answers to our problems are closer than we think."

*

Alone now, Jack gingerly moved the blankets back. Embarrassingly, someone had taken his trousers off and he was in his boxer shorts. He looked at the new bandage on his leg and slowly started undoing the dressing. Cautiously he lifted off the gauze pad and inspected his shin. Pus oozed out of the long slit and had stained the pad yellow. He shuddered as he replaced the bandage. It made him feel sick looking at it.

What an idiot he was for getting so carried away with his theory about Dad. And he felt a deep shame. How could he have believed Dad was involved in something so wrong? And how had he got so sidetracked? He'd wasted precious time – time he didn't have. His skin was not going to get better on its own – his leg throbbed as if in agreement. He still had to find Dad. And there was only one person who could help him do that.

There was a click of heels on the floor and the curtain swished open as Mum appeared. Relief washed over him and he beamed as she gave him a hug.

"Thank goodness you're all right. I've been worried sick since Auntie Lil called me – I came as soon as I could. I've brought you some magazines and your iPod from Lil's." By the way she slapped them on his bedside table and plonked herself in the chair by his bed Jack

179

knew he was in for a lecture. "What on earth possessed you – first going off without telling me, then climbing onto the lab roof? You're lucky Dr Blackstone's so understanding and is not going to press charges. Very lucky, in fact."

"Sorry," he mumbled. "I wanted to find Dad."

"I didn't realise how badly you wanted to see him. I should have listened to you properly, taken more notice. And why didn't you talk to me about your skin? Not left it to Lil to tell me."

"You seemed so worried about money and everything."

"I've been a bit preoccupied lately, but you can always talk to me, whatever's on your mind. And things will be different from now on. Your dad's got in touch again and he'll be coming to see you when we get home."

"You've found him?"

Mum reached out and ruffled his hair. "He was never really lost. He just didn't think how his actions would affect you."

Jack grinned with delight.

"And I've found a great skin specialist and she wants to meet you," continued Mum. "We'll get on top of this, you'll see."

"I've had enough of being prodded and poked by doctors. Fat lot of good it's done." All he needed was a stronger sun lotion. Didn't she get that? "Dad can help me."

Mum peered at him and sighed. "He can certainly start acting like a proper dad."

She squeezed his hand and stood up. "Listen, Jack. I thought you realised how bad things were between your dad and me . . . what with all the arguing."

"I didn't think it was that serious," he mumbled.

"I owe you a decent explanation about everything when you get out of here. But there's someone outside who's very eager to see you. I'll grab a coffee and send her in."

Mum disappeared through the curtain. Grunting, Jack stretched out a hand towards the magazines. Unable to reach, he clambered out of the bed, unclipping the pulse monitor. Immediately the machine gave an angry beep. Ignoring it, he shuffled over to the chair and picked up the top magazine, *Street Sport*. Funny Mum had chosen that one for him, when she didn't have a clue what he did on the roofs.

He was about to hop back into bed when his attention was caught by the front cover of the magazine underneath. Mum must have picked it up from Auntie Lil's by mistake. "Factors Effecting Photosensitivity" read the headline of Beth's *Junior Medical Monthly*.

Clambering back into bed and re-clipping the pulse monitor on before a nurse could appear to tell him off, he thumbed through the magazine until he found the article.

He stared at the words so long and hard they started to blur in front of his eyes. His brain refused to take in what he was reading. At last, he sank back on the pillows, the magazine falling with a thud to the floor.

Chapter Twenty-Four

The word "psychosomatic" bounced around inside his head like the silver ball in a pinball machine. He picked the magazine up again and tried to focus on what the article said – that some physical conditions and diseases could be made worse by mental factors, such as stress and anxiety. There was that word again: "stress". Could that be him?

When exactly had the first sore appeared? It'd been *before* Dad had gone away – hadn't it? He searched the deepest niches of his brain. And then he remembered. His symptoms had started on his birthday, a few months after Dad left. When Dad had sent a short email – an email that hadn't even said happy birthday. And it was then that the first seeds of doubt about whether he was ever coming back had been sown. After that, the sores kept popping up. Each one worse than the last. Then there'd been the wound on his hand and the sore behind his ear. And of course, his leg – he cast his mind back to when he'd found that sore. It was after the visit to the library. When Mum told him about the separation and seeing the solicitor. Words from the magazine article trickled through his head; had worrying about Dad made his photosensitivity worse? Was it possible for anxiety to have such an impact on his skin?

He thought back to what Dr Blackstone had said: *Sometimes the answers to our problems are closer than we think.* Perhaps stress was to blame. And all the investigations he and Beth had done would have piled on more stress. He swallowed the lump that had appeared in his throat. Did he need a stronger lotion? Or was his dilapidated skin a result of his mind playing tricks on his body? He didn't know what to believe any more.

A head appeared between the two curtains and Beth sidled into the cubicle, rucksack in her hand. He gave her a watery grin, glad to see a friendly face.

"Hi," she said.

"Hi yourself." Beth's hair was a mess, flattened to her scalp and drooping over the left side of her face. Grey streaks marked her cheeks and dirty shadows surrounded each eye. Exhaustion was stamped on her features. She looked as bad as he felt. "How's things?" he asked.

"I'm in trouble with Cathy. Nothing I can't handle though," she said, as she sat on the edge of his bed, her knee touching his thigh. "Feeling any better?"

Jack shrugged. He attempted another smile and then grimaced as a sharp pain scooted across his bashed forehead. "Not bad. See you've got your rucksack back."

"Dr Blackstone gave it to me," she said, twisting her fingers through the straps. Unease seemed to ooze out of her and an awkward silence stretched between them. "So, you'll be able to leave soon your mum says. And at least you can stop looking for your dad."

"Yeah," he said. "I feel a bit of an idiot now. Getting obsessed with it all."

Her eyes flitted to the magazine lying on the bed and back to Jack. "You've found the article then," she said quietly. "Does it make sense?"

"This?" he said, confused. Then the cogs in his brain creaked into action as he looked from the magazine in his hand to Beth. A vague memory stirred of her reading *Junior Medical Monthly* at Auntie Lil's. At the time she'd been cagey about it and he'd wondered why. "Wait a minute. You knew about this 'psychosomatic' disorder?"

She gave him a long look, a tinge of pink colouring

each grey cheek. Then she nodded, lips pressed together in a thin line. "When I first met you on the roofs, I remembered reading about it in my magazine."

"Why didn't you show it to me?" An icy tickle scuttled down his spine as he stared at Beth's grey-white face and grappled with the idea that she'd known about the article all along.

"I told you worry might be making your skin worse, I'm sure I did." Her voice faltered. Suddenly she looked unsure of herself. "Before we went to the lab last night. You didn't want to know."

Jack's skull buzzed unpleasantly. He'd been too caught up in his plan to get into the labs to take much notice of what she was saying. Maybe she had told him, but it was too little, too late. Hurt throbbed in the veins under his fragile skin. She'd pushed him to investigate Dad's disappearance – egged him on. She'd suggested they visit Auntie Lil, talk to Ted, meet Blackstone. Why do that if she thought it would make him worse? He felt giddy, as if all the air had been sucked out of his lungs by a huge vacuum pump. "You should have told me before things went so far."

The features on her face seemed to collapse in on themselves. "When you suggested getting into the lab I said it was a bad idea. I tried to stop you."

"You didn't try very hard, did you?"

"I . . . I didn't know things would get that bad. I thought there might be a link between your dad leaving and your skin, but I wasn't sure. It's not something I could prove."

Jack suddenly realised why she had quizzed Dr Blackstone about stress. Not because of Dad but because of his skin.

"You seemed so sure you needed a new lotion. And I didn't think for a minute everything would turn out the way it did . . . I'm sorry."

"You should have shown me the article," he repeated.

She paused a beat. "Like you should have told me about the ashes."

"Oh, I get it – so this is some kind of payback."

"No, it's not, Jack. I'm not like that."

Jack's embarrassment and upset spilled out of him. What an idiot he'd been – to believe he'd found someone who really "got" him.

"You know what I think? You've been trying to forget your own problems by focusing on mine." He knew he was going too far, but somehow he couldn't stop himself.

Beth gazed at her hands in her lap. "I wanted to help you."

"Stop interfering in my life and sort your own out. You

need to face facts – your parents are dead and nothing will bring them back."

As soon as those furious words left his mouth a fistful of guilt and sadness punched the anger away. "Sorry" formed on his lips but it was too late. Her face was frozen and closed. Not meeting his eyes, she grabbed her bag and stuffed the magazine inside. He stretched out a hand to hold her back but she darted out of reach. He turned away, his eyes prickling with unshed tears and as he listened to the curtain swishing open he stifled a moan. He didn't understand what had been going on. Had she used him as a distraction? If so, could he really blame her? She was damaged, like him. He had to take some responsibility for his actions because not everything was her fault.

Chapter Twenty-Five

Two weeks later

Jack stood on the shady side of the chimney, scrunching up his eyes as he gazed over the tops of the roofs to the cathedral. With an angry lurch, he flung back his arm and launched a fragment of roof tile in the air. It curved high and then skittered down the slope, bouncing off the guttering and disappearing over the edge.

He looked up at the sky. It had turned a weird colour. Along with the different shades of orange and yellow, dark clouds had built up, like angry, grey blobs of candy floss hanging over the city. Rays from the sun filtered around the clouds, striking the surrounding buildings. The muggy, oppressive air sapped his energy, the heaviness making it difficult to take a breath. The weather was changing; after weeks of torrid heat there was going to be one hell of a storm. As if to confirm his thought he heard a distant rumble.

A sigh escaped him as he readied himself for the next leap. He shook his legs and rolled his shoulders to loosen the muscles. Then he took a running jump from the shadow, arms outstretched. He landed with his hands grasping the top of a wall and his feet gripping the brickwork. Hauling himself up and over, he came to rest in the shade on the other side, panting slightly.

Every day dragged endlessly, waiting for a call at the flat or expecting Beth's spiky head to poke round one of the chimneys. Two weeks had passed since they'd argued at the hospital. Two long weeks since he'd seen or spoken to her. He'd hoped spending time in his favourite place would help him forget her for a while. But it wasn't working. Shadow jumping didn't feel the same. He went through the motions but something was missing.

Beth.

He missed her more than he thought possible.

Things at home had improved, though. Well, they made more sense, anyway. He'd seen Dad, and both he and Mum had explained properly that they would be formally separating. Things hadn't been right between them for ages, he recognised that now. Dad had been suffering from stress on and off for years. That explained the mood swings. But at last he'd asked for and was getting the help he needed from doctors. Everyone needed a fresh start, so Mum and Dad said. Dad had even said sorry for not phoning. He promised never to do that again and Jack believed him.

Aberdeen – that's where Dad's new job was. He couldn't live further away if he tried, but he'd told Jack he'd fly down some weekends and Jack could spend the school holidays with him. And, as Dad joked, they didn't get a lot of sun in Aberdeen, so his photosensitivity shouldn't be too much of a problem.

Jack tentatively touched the scab behind his ear and reached into his pocket for his cream. He dabbed some on his face. His skin was slowly getting better, but he wasn't using a new lotion. Seeing Dad again after all those months was like having a hefty weight lifted from his shoulders. Looking back, it did seem as if the more he missed Dad the worse his fragile skin had got. But it wasn't easy to prove worry was responsible. He'd probably never know for sure.

Even though Dad reckoned he didn't need a new suncream, he wanted Jack to see the specialist, in case there were better treatments available. Jack agreed; anything for a quiet life.

Trouble was life was too quiet, thought Jack, as he rammed the lid on the tube and set it beside him on the tiles. Enough was enough. Time to mend some bridges. He rooted in his pocket and brought out Mum's phone.

*

"Hey, you."

Jack raised his head. Tiny pieces of debris bounced down the tiles towards him as Beth appeared a couple of metres away. She wore her usual black leggings and T-shirt, her make-up as startling as ever.

"Hey," said Jack.

She scooted down the slope and sat beside him, taking her rucksack off and placing it between her knees.

"I'm glad you came," he said.

"To tell you the truth, I nearly didn't," she mumbled as she toyed with her rucksack. "I should have told you about the article. But I admit a big part of me didn't want you to stop the search. And you're right – looking for your dad did take my mind off my own problems and it was fun to start with. Until it all turned serious. Then, I couldn't find the words to tell you what I'd read."

"It's okay. I've got a brain – I didn't need to agree with everything you suggested." He cleared his throat. "And I'm sorry, you know, for not telling you about the ashes."

Beth edged nearer to Jack, looping the straps of her

192

bag over her knees. Jack grinned – it was great to see her. Great to see her black-lined eyes creased at the corners and her lips quirked upwards in a tentative smile.

"So, what now?"

"I've got an idea," he said. "Want to do some jumping?"

Beth beamed. "I got the feeling you didn't want me up here."

He gave an embarrassed laugh. "Yeah, well. That was before, you know, everything. I've learnt some things are even better when they're shared. It's not the same without you." He pulled her to her feet. "But we haven't got long. It's going to rain."

"Let's have a race then."

Jack raised an eyebrow. She had to be joking. "I'll win."

"Don't be so sure. I've been practising."

He shrugged. He knew the roofs like the back of his scabby hand. No way was she better than him, but he wasn't going to argue.

"The race finishes there," she said, pointing to a distinctive, tall, ornate chimney in the distance.

"You'll have to leave that here." He gestured at the rucksack Beth still had in her hand. "We can pick it up on the way back."

"I don't know . . ." said Beth, clutching it to her chest.

"It'll be safe here. You can't jump properly with it." He held out his hand and slowly she handed it to him. He lodged it against the upper side of the chimney where they sat.

They lined up on a flat section of the roof as the first drops of rain landed around them. Beth looked at Jack and he gave her a small smile of encouragement. His insides started to churn with nervous anticipation.

"Ready, go!" shouted Beth.

They sped along the asphalted roof, rounded a corner and leapt over a low wall. As Jack raced up a steep pitch with Beth, he could already feel himself pulling in front. He reached the top and got a tantalising view, through the fine drizzle, of the finish, before slithering down the other side and heaving himself over a wall. Jack glanced back to see Beth not far behind.

Within a matter of seconds the rain became torrential. It hammered around him, streaming past and over his feet, towards the guttering. He was soaked. The water seeped into his trainers; each step he took made them squelch. Above, the sky was dark and heavy, lit occasionally by vivid flashes of lightning. Booms and crashes of thunder followed.

Jack looked back. Water streamed down Beth's face

and plastered her hair to her scalp. Black rivulets flowed down her cheeks where her eye make-up had dissolved. Her teeth chattered like his own.

He spotted a small brick overhang. "We need to get undercover! This way!" he shouted, straining to be heard above the pounding rain.

Grabbing Beth's arm, he clawed his way up a slope, feet and fingers sliding on the sopping tiles. He knew they were exposed and vulnerable on the roof. The race was all but forgotten.

"My bag," screamed Beth, as she twisted round to set off back the way they'd come. "It'll get wet."

"It's too slippery." Jack tried to grasp her arm once more but she wrestled it out of reach.

He shouted again but the cascading water drowned out his words. He watched as she vaulted over a wall. He leapt after her.

His foot caught on something and he stumbled into a puddle of rainwater. He staggered to his knees but made it no further as something hard slammed into his ribs. The pain was unbearable – as if his lungs had been pulled through his throat. Through blurred eyes he looked around. Fuzzy shapes appeared, and stripes. His pulse quickened. Deckchairs. He must have leapt onto the roof terrace. A figure loomed over him. Kai.

He lurched onto his knees, clutching his side.

"You again," sneered Kai. "Where's your freaky girlfriend?"

"She's not up here." Jack took a breath and winced as a sharp ache pierced his ribs.

"See, I don't believe you. You need to learn to stay away from here."

As Jack struggled to get up Beth appeared. She crept up behind Kai. Time seemed to stand still as Jack watched her manoeuvre the rucksack off her back. Holding the straps in both hands, she swung it once and brought it up to hit Kai on his oversized head. His legs buckled under him and he fell. It was like watching the demolition of an industrial chimney. "Who's gonna make us?" she said.

She held out a hand and helped Jack to his feet. Wasting no time they hurtled down the next slope, putting distance between them and Kai. Cascades of water flowed around them. They vaulted over metal railings and landed on a gently sloping roof. Jack prayed that the tiles wouldn't be so slippery that they'd slide straight off the edge. He looked back. A dark shape followed, getting closer. Kai. He ran faster, dragging Beth along behind him. A deep pain pierced his chest as he struggled to get enough breath into his lungs. Just in time he spotted the end of the roof looming. A low parapet marked the edge.

Jack teetered on the brink, almost losing his balance, before steadying himself and stepping away from the drop. He squinted into the gloom – the chimney was not far.

"We've got to jump."

"I c-can't." Her breath came in juddering gasps. Her arm shook under his hand. Snot dribbled out of her nose.

"We're nearly there. You can do this, Beth. Trust me."

Kai appeared on the ridge.

She held out her wet hand and he gave it a brief squeeze. They took a few paces and jumped together.

Chapter Twenty-Six

Every taut muscle in his body sang out with the thrill of the leap. Adrenaline pulsed through his blood. The soles of his feet felt as if they'd explode from the pressure of the landing, which was a perfect one, despite the rain. The chimney marking the finish stood above him, one short sprint away.

"We've done it!" he shouted to Beth, wiping his soaked fringe out of his eyes.

She wasn't standing next to him. Fear seemed to squeeze the air out of his body. He scampered to the edge and peered over into the murkiness, panic and raindrops blurring his vision.

Bending down he saw white fingers clutching the gutter. He clasped the hand and pulled.

"My bag." Beth's breath came in juddering gasps as he heaved her upwards. It was then Jack noticed the rucksack straps clenched in her other hand, her arm stretched taut by the weight, down by her side. "I can't hold onto it."

"Let it go," he shouted. "It's too heavy."

"No."

"Don't be so stupid. Do you want to die?" In that split second he realised she'd rather fall than let go. He fumbled with the sodden rucksack and prised it from her hand. He chucked it onto the slates behind him. Then he tugged Beth up the roof, inch by inch, until she lay like a damp rag, eyes half closed, make-up all but washed away. He flopped onto his back, his chest heaving with exhaustion.

"The ashes." Beth suddenly sat up, a wild look in her eyes.

Jack's heart gave a sickening thud. The bag lay where he'd thrown it. It gaped open. The wooden boxes were a metre away. They rested on their sides, lids ajar, clasps bashed and broken. All that remained of the contents were soppy, grey streaks flowing down the tiles.

Beth crawled over on her hands and knees.

"No!" she sobbed, kneeling by the muddy rivulet as she attempted to scoop the spillage up.

"Stop. It's no use, they're gone." He couldn't bear to see her scrabbling about in the dirt. He felt terrible – it was his fault. "I'm sorry."

Beth sat back on her heels and raised her face to the sky, eyes closed. Jack didn't know what to do – what was there to say? He'd lost her parents' ashes. The most important thing in her life – gone.

She uttered a huge, trembling moan, then fell silent. Jack sat miserably next to her.

At last she turned to him. "Let's finish the race."

"Really?" he asked, his voice quivering. "Are you sure?"

She nodded.

He looped his arm around her waist. "We'll do it together then," he said.

Half carrying her, he set off up the roof towards the chimney, not stopping until he could touch the wet brickwork. Then he carefully propped her against the stack and sat next to her, holding her hand. Neither of them spoke.

Kai had disappeared; Jack was sure he hadn't seen the last of him, but it didn't matter any more. They were safe for now and that was enough.

For the first time he noticed the rain had stopped, the clouds having rolled away on a cool breeze. End of the day sunlight reflected off the saturated tiles surrounding where they sat, and a hazy rainbow had appeared over the cathedral tower. Water trickled and dribbled into the gutters around them. The distant whoosh of traffic splashing through rain puddles drifted up to them from the road.

"Sorry about the ashes," he said. "If I'd known they'd spill—"

"What? You'd have rescued them instead of me?" Beth gazed at him. "You did the right thing. I thought I was a goner there. Thanks for saving me."

"Just repaying the favour." He grinned, relief making him giddy.

"I've been thinking." Beth brought her knees up to her chest and wrapped her arms round them. "There's something I need to do. Will you help me?"

Jack nodded; it was not the time for words. Instead, he put an arm across her shoulders and hugged her.

Chapter Twenty-Seven

Jack stood on the edge of the grassy cliff looking out to sea. The sky was a bright blue; small, fluffy, cotton-wool clouds floated past and the far off swish of the waves was interrupted by the screaming seagulls, circling above. Below him the grey, shiny rocks gave way to the golden sands of Witcombe Beach.

The sun pounded onto his covered scalp. For a moment a twinge of fear took hold and then he relaxed. It would take him a while to learn not to panic the second he stepped into the sun. He couldn't believe how quickly his skin had improved in the last few weeks. Even his leg was better. A pale pink scar ran down his shin, but that would soon disappear. He'd never be able to spend much time in the sun and he'd still have to wear lotion when outside.

But, hey, there were worse things in life.

He thought back to a few weeks ago, to shadow jumping and meeting Beth up on the roofs. How much had changed for him since then. He looked at the girl standing next to him. Beth had also changed. Gone was the thick black and white make-up. Without it, her face looked softer somehow. One day he'd tell her that.

They'd always be different to other kids. Most kids hadn't been through what they'd been through; they hadn't lost their parents or had to put up with a devastating skin condition. But he was stronger now and he was sure Beth felt the same way too. School would be starting next week and for once dread didn't fill his every waking moment.

"Ready?" he asked.

Beth nodded and reached into her rucksack. One by one she pulled out the battered urns. Jack held one of them so that Beth could open the lid of the other. As she tipped the box upside down, instead of ashes, a shower of petals drifted out. Whisked upwards on an eddy of wind, they floated over the cliff on the breeze. The pink rose – her mother's favourite flower. The flower her dad picked from the garden on the day of the picnic at the beach.

As she opened the other box and shook the petals out, she sighed.

"I reckon my mum and dad would have been glad you chose me to save rather than their remains. And they'll always be with me. In here." She tapped her chest with a finger. "What's this, by the way?" She stopped and dug around in the bag, pulling out the glass paperweight he'd put in her rucksack at Auntie Lil's.

"Ah," he said. "I can explain . . ."

"No need. I can guess."

In the distance a dusty cloud moved along the road towards them. "Bus's coming," said Jack.

"Race you!" said Beth, as she sprinted towards the bus stop, her black hair bobbing in the breeze.

"Oi! That's not fair." Jack grinned as he tore after her.

Some things would never change.

Write a review!

Let the author know what you thought of *Shadow Jumper* by visiting **www.jm-forster.co.uk** and filling in the contact form.

You can keep up-to-date with Julia's news on her website too!

About the Author

J M Forster spends her daylight hours talking to teenagers about their futures, but at night she turns into a writer of books for older children and young teens. She lives in Gloucestershire with her husband and two lovely sons.

Shadow Jumper is her first novel.

www.jm-forster.co.uk

22378114R00124

Printed in Great Britain
by Amazon